AMERICAN DELIRIUM

AMERICAN DELIRIUM

BETINA GONZÁLEZ

Translated by
Heather Cleary

Henry Holt and Company   New York

Henry Holt and Company
Publishers since 1866
120 Broadway
New York, NY 10271
www.henryholt.com

Henry Holt® and 🂠® are registered trademarks of
Macmillan Publishing Group, LLC.

Originally published in Argentina and Spain in 2016
under the title *América alucinada*
by Tusquets Argentina and Tusquets Editores

Library of Congress Cataloging-in-Publication Data

Names: González, Betina, 1972– author. | Cleary, Heather, translator.
Title: American delirium / Betina González ; translated by Heather Cleary.
Other titles: América alucinada. English
Description: First U.S. edition. | New York : Henry Holt and Company, 2021.
| Originally published in Argentina and Spain in 2016 under the title
América alucinada by Tusquets Editores S.A.
Identifiers: LCCN 2020018806 (print) | LCCN 2020018807 (ebook)
| ISBN 9781250621283 (hardcover) | ISBN 9781250621269 (ebook)
Classification: LCC PQ7798.417.O59 A8413 2021 (print) | LCC PQ7798.417.O59
(ebook) | DDC 863/.7—dc23
LC record available at https://lccn.loc.gov/2020018806
LC ebook record available at https://lccn.loc.gov/2020018807

Our books may be purchased in bulk for promotional,
educational, or business use. Please contact your local
bookseller or the Macmillan Corporate and Premium Sales
Department at (800) 221-7945, extension 5442, or by e-mail at
MacmillanSpecialMarkets@macmillan.com.

First U.S. Edition 2021

Designed by Meryl Sussman Levavi

Printed in the United States of America

1   2   3   4   5   6   7   8   9   10

What you have to do is enter the fiction of
  America, enter America as fiction.
It is, indeed, on this fictive basis that it dominates
  the world.

—Jean Baudrillard
America

AMERICAN DELIRIUM

1

The day he found a woman hiding in his closet, Vik had dreamt about winning a Ping-Pong tournament. The two events were unrelated, aside from the nearly identical feeling they produced: triumph followed by disgust. The way he'd sneaked into his own home and stealthily pressed his ear to the closet door was exactly like the perfectly calculated arc of his arm as he flicked the ball beyond his opponent's reach.

Just then, with the suspense of those days nearly at its end, his ear registered—despite the two inches of oak that separated him from his discovery—a loud peal of laughter. Vik lurched back from the closet door as if it had given him an electric shock, losing his balance. That was when he remembered the dream. Especially the face of his opponent, an older man who kept taking off his glasses to wipe the sweat from his face with his forearm. As the spectators cheered, the man shook his head slowly, wondering how this ten-year-old boy could have beaten him at his favorite game.

Vik, who had never played Ping-Pong and was exactly forty-one years old, had woken up feeling sick, or swindled, as if he'd just come out of a routine operation to find that one of his organs had been removed without his consent. Luckily, his brain was equipped with dozens of chemical defense mechanisms that set about erasing the images, along with the bitter discomfort they produced, as soon as Vik stepped out of the shower. He knew what he needed to do. He dried off and put on his clothes, a slight twinge of apprehension lingering in his chest. He left the house at quarter to eight as he always did, but not before checking the windows and the complex surveillance system he'd installed the day before.

The system wasn't really all that complex. But his complete technological illiteracy had forced him to hire someone to install it. There were two cameras, one in the kitchen and another in the hallway between the bedroom and the bathroom, which sent images straight to his cell phone. The technician—who had a storefront on Grandville—congratulated him, saying that many homeowners were choosing to become their own security guards. "You never know what happens after you close that front door," he'd said, shaking Vik's hand harder than necessary.

Vik hadn't even owned a cell phone a few days earlier. Now he had one with an empty contacts folder. He always used to wonder what could be so urgent that people felt compelled to drive with that little device stuck to their necks, or to risk letting some burial plot salesman interrupt their enjoyment of a sunny day. Now he understood. Now he was one of them. What next? Eating in a restaurant? The idea made his skin crawl. Stepping into some dining hall full of people wolfing down their lunches, or one of those places where they played classical music in a futile attempt to drown out the sound of forty or fifty jaws working in unison . . . No. That would definitely be too much.

The first day, he forgot about the whole thing and the phone sat in his jacket pocket. It wasn't until it rang, exaggeratedly loud in the quiet of his workshop, that he remembered it was there. It was the technician who'd installed the cameras—who else would it be?—calling to see if everything was all right. "Everything's fine," Vik lied. He'd just noticed, in the video feed from his kitchen, that a piece of bread he'd intentionally left on the table that morning was gone. The problem was that he'd placed it at the very edge of the camera's range, which meant he needed to strain to detect its absence in the image on his cell phone screen. The thief had taken the bait, but remained outside the frame. Alongside his frustration, Vik felt a touch of relief. He still hadn't figured out what he was going to do when he caught this person. What he really wanted was to get rid of the phone, right then and there. But he left it on his workstation instead, hypnotized by the blue glow of the screen.

Still thinking about the device, he got back to work on the snake he'd been repairing all month. Boxes of old Ploucquet dioramas and donations from other museums were piling up on a big wooden table. Anyone could see he was falling behind. He'd been arriving at the workshop with barely any energy lately and had a hard time concentrating. He was surprised that Miss Beryl hadn't mentioned it yet. What would she say if she found out he had a cell phone now, too? She'd ask all kinds of questions, make all kinds of assumptions.

The others hung on Miss Beryl's every word. They seemed to think there was something naturally clever about the old bag, even though she did nothing but talk about what she'd seen on television, her childhood in the mountains, and other people's lives—garnished with a dash of practical Darwinism, a strong dose of mistrust for anyone with a passport or a university degree, and a pathetic nostalgia for good old days that weren't coming back. Miss Beryl was a disaster waiting to happen. One little slip and minutes later the whole museum would know that someone was breaking into his house and stealing his food. Even bathing in his tub.

Vik wasn't sure exactly when it had begun. A few nights ago, probably, when he got home from the gym and noticed that the house smelled like sandalwood. He didn't remember lighting incense before he left. Nor did he like sandalwood. After much searching, he'd eventually found a box of incense on one of the sofas, but he didn't think much of it and headed for the shower. The walk from the bus station had been an ordeal, even though it was only a few blocks. It was raining, which always slowed him down. He preferred to take his time, rather than risk making a false move with his cane and falling in front of the neighbors. Especially since he insisted on wearing leather shoes, which really weren't suited to the climate. His doctor had suggested he try something "more appropriate." What did he expect? For him to start wearing those horrible trainers that teenagers put on their feet to feel faster, stronger, tougher?

Vik knew that, just like the pill bottles on his nightstand and the half hour of exercises he suffered through daily, it was all simply meant to help his doctors sleep at night. The fact was that his nervous system had been deteriorating for years and no one knew why. He had a collection of ultrasounds that showed bits of connective tissue floating at random around his spinal column. They looked like malevolent little creatures, or fish. Like part of some alternative design his body had decided to adopt: intelligent, translucent lines composing the sharp and bottomless shape of the word "pain."

Vik knew the exercises were useless, but he followed the doctors' instructions to the letter. He liked walking as much as anyone, and he wanted to be able to keep doing it. He was so tired when he left the gym, though, that he would need to take the bus the twelve blocks home. This invariably put him in a bad mood. He had no patience for the obese passengers who took up two seats, the senior citizens in wheelchairs, the homeless, or the nutters who prayed at the top of their lungs. The scent of decay, of a city collapsing under neon lights, clung to them.

He should have realized it that night. But he was so tired he didn't even have the strength to make himself dinner. As he was getting out of the shower, he'd felt something vaguely repulsive brush against his heel. He'd jerked his foot back so quickly he almost lost his balance. Once the tub emptied, the circular metal of the drain revealed the culprit: a soapy coil of long black hair. He didn't have the courage to crouch down and examine it up close. He ran a hand over his head to make sure he hadn't suddenly lost a huge tuft. If his body had decided to shed neural fibers, why not hair as well? In the end, he decided it had to be lint or accumulated grime. He promised himself he'd clean the place properly soon. He stuck a morphine patch on his right shoulder, put on his headphones to listen to the sounds of the ocean, and got into bed, as he always did, at eight thirty.

Cleaning wasn't one of his priorities. He rarely had energy to spare on housework. He preferred to save it for his clothing, which he made sure was always impeccable. He'd trained himself in recent years to keep his disarray to a minimum. Everything was immediately put away after use; he could swear he ate every meal from the same plate, with the same fork. Not to say that a lone shoe didn't occasionally turn up under the sofa or behind a chair, as a sign of one of those days his strength had left him too soon. The air that filtered through his home was as stagnant and dark as his wooden furniture, as the essential oils in the diffuser by the front door. A fine layer of dust had settled over the rooms, from the photographs of his parents on the bookshelf in the dining room, to the small colonial silver teacups on the coffee table. He occasionally considered hiring a maid, but ultimately decided it was an unnecessary expense.

Morning was his favorite time of day. It was when he felt powerful. The ten and a half hours of sleep managed to fool his body for a while, and he woke up full of love for the world. At least, for the gray sky hanging over the city, the birds singing despite the cold, and the snow falling like a gift onto his windowsill. He didn't get out of bed right away. He'd lie there watching the news or just thinking, sometimes still caught in the remains of a dream. At seven, he'd get up and go to the kitchen for some cereal or fruit. He would read for a while. Take a shower. He'd choose his clothes carefully, sometimes trying on one or two different outfits before deciding, and then head to the café on the corner, where he always ordered the same thing: a large black coffee with extra sugar.

All this had probably made him an easy target. He realized that now. There was probably no one in the world with a routine as rigid as his. He always came home at the same time. Always took the same streets. No one ever visited him, except his brother. But that was only once or twice a year, when Prasad took a break between business trips and drove the twelve hours that separated them. He considered the possibility that the whole thing was a joke. But whose? The idea that someone might see him as a victim enraged him. Far more than the thefts he'd noticed over the four days following his encounter with the clump of hair. It was always fruit or bread. Or milk. Lately, a bottle hardly lasted a day or two, and then there was the time half of a bunch of grapes he'd bought on his way home from the gym just disappeared. There were crumbs in his bed. And he couldn't find one of his towels (pink with yellow stitching) anywhere.

It was just a matter of figuring out which window the thief was using to break in. He'd considered installing grates, but that would ruin the house's appearance. But what if the intruder had a key? He'd heard stories of people who became obsessed with places they'd lived in before. People who lost their minds and returned to their childhood homes as if time had stood still. He'd changed the lock, but the idea was too unsettling to be dismissed with a reassuring thought or two. He might have preferred to discover that he was going crazy. That would have been much better. Then he wouldn't need to worry about securing the windows every time he went out, and he wouldn't have needed to hire that technician to install security cameras.

Because now he had a red cell phone that could ring at any moment. Now he was falling behind in his work and was always in a bad mood. Now the simple act of getting into bed at night was like stepping into a torture chamber. Now he obsessively reviewed the contents of his refrigerator, stayed longer at the gym, and let several buses pass before finally deciding it was time to go home. Anyone could see that he wasn't sleeping well, that every little noise startled him, and that the mornings didn't find him full of love for the world anymore.

Where was all this headed? Only one thing was certain: he'd become the kind of man who spied on his own home.

☞

My first deer still had its spots. I killed it with a Marlin 336. I didn't know it at the time, but the spots meant that the animal was less than six months old. It's illegal to hunt them when they're that young, but Dad didn't mention that part. He congratulated me and rubbed my shoulder, right where the rifle had left a dark blue bruise over days of practice.

It was years before I went back to it. So much can happen to a girl in a city like this. Especially when you get to be a certain age. People wrinkle their noses as they pass, like they can smell the thousands of dead cells you're carrying inside, the microscopic trail you leave behind like a slug. But it's not true. Not everything inside me is rotting. Sometimes I'd like to prove them right, though. There's nothing worse than having someone hand your fears to you gift-wrapped. Why not show them what's waiting around the bend? Most of them act like they're immortal. Like they've got all the time in the world to decide between the skim milk and the kind with two percent fat and all the vitamins they'll need to delay the moment they need to start wearing diapers again. Sometimes I'm tempted to do something awful, like stop the chick coming my way with her kid in a shopping cart and scream right in his freckled little face. To him, I'm just a Halloween mask or a pile of dirty clothes someone forgot to pick up. I've considered (I consider) worse. At the very least, someone should teach them a few survival skills. The average family in this country wastes twenty-five pounds of food per year. Fact. And that's not even counting the tons of garbage they produce. They think they can make it all better by putting their newspapers and magazines in a little blue bin every night, their glass bottles in a red one, and everything else in the trash. Then they go to sleep and dream of buying a bigger house, having their picture in one of those magazines, spicing things up with the old ball and chain. They're like little kids. Wouldn't last two hours on their own. In the morning, they hop in their giant pickup trucks and forget all about it.

When the deer started attacking people, no one thought it was important enough to put on the news. Only a few of us saw it for what it was: another sign of our weakness. The rest just went on planting their tomatoes, making sure they got enough fiber, and keeping up with events in the Middle East. They didn't react, not even when the deer started coming in droves. Their faith in the assurances of ecologists, in the government, and in their weekly salsa lessons never wavered. They probably read about what happened to Ron Duda the way you might read about the genetic mutation of a fly in some remote tropical region, or an exotic disease that—thank God—only affects people with one eye, or those of us constantly on the verge of falling off society's radar. It didn't occur to them that Duda could be their neighbor, another moron whose fences and intercoms failed to protect from their love of nature.

Ron Duda had a house right at the edge of the woods, a wife as fragile as tissue paper, and too much time on his hands. Who knows whether it was an attempt to stay active or to impress his friends with homemade pasta sauce, but he also had a little garden where he grew tomatoes, basil, and eggplant. He spent hours out there every week, trying to keep the woods at bay. The woods, of course, insisted on expanding far beyond his plans for it, which were limited to appearing in the thirty-two watercolors his wife had painted from their dining room and providing the setting for monthly educational excursions to the river so his grandkids could get their hands dirty and learn that not everything good and beautiful in the world comes with a barcode. The good Mr. Duda was probably lost in thoughts of this caliber, squatting over his hundred-percent-organic tomatoes, when he was ambushed by a six-point buck.

He didn't even have time to stand up. One point of the

animal's antler tore his cheek to the bone, and another went in through his mouth. A blood clot formed on the spot and started making its way to his lungs. Duda dragged himself from his vegetable beds toward the glass doors of the dining room, where his wife had just poured two bowls of cereal. He died in the hospital three days later, from the clot. His wife said the deer was over five feet tall and had a scar on its neck.

No one thought to look for the animal, though they did reroute school buses, and a few people from the neighborhood set up a patrol. A couple of days later, the whole thing had been forgotten. But some of us were getting ready.

In a city where deer had outnumbered humans for years, it didn't take long for other reports to start coming in. One doe bit a young woman in the parking lot of a shopping mall as she was getting into her car. The woman tried to defend herself with an umbrella, but the deer trampled her shopping bags, broke her bottles of wrinkle cream, decimated her centerpieces, and made off with a chunk of the woman's arm between its teeth. Several university students blamed bruises, broken bones, and tardiness on attacks during lunch in the parks around campus. The authorities considered restricting access to the city's cemeteries, which had been overrun for a long time already. Graveside ambushes are so common that no one even bothers to report them anymore. Some people visit their departed armed with sticks. Others are too scared to get out of their cars, so they toss their flowers and their prayers out the window as they pass. On the other end of the city, at least one runner and one cyclist were attacked by a doe that didn't seem to think Four Winds Avenue was a good place for humans to burn their calories. And so it goes.

None of these cases, though, was as sensational as Emilia Bourdette's. While Ron Duda didn't even make the local news,

Emilia sparked waves of protests across the city. The incident occurred before Duda was attacked. It was the middle of summer. Emilia's roses and petunias were in bloom, and hundreds of fawns had just been born. One morning, she stepped out into her garden to find two of her flower beds completely destroyed, and the culprit—a fawn no more than a few months old—sitting comfortably on a third. The animal didn't bat an eye when it saw her coming, which made Emilia, a southerner "accustomed to dealing with all manner of pests," even angrier. A city girl would have reacted differently. But Emilia lifted her shovel and brought it down square on the fawn's head. She couldn't stop. She beat the animal until it was nothing but a mass of flesh, fur, and blood mixed in among the yellow petals.

She never did figure out who called the police. In a neighborhood like ours, full of seniors with too much free time, it's not hard to imagine what happened. Anyway, it's not like Emilia was ever all that popular around here. She's one of those women who shakes the family tree every time you talk to her until a French duke or two with last names like salad dressings falls out, sometimes followed by a famous writer. The police questioned her for hours, and eventually charged her with animal cruelty. Protests were organized. Groups of young people marched in front of the Fish and Wildlife offices with signs demanding the maximum sentence (a fine and two months of community service). Others papered the neighborhood with posters featuring a picture of Bambi above the words "Don't kill me, Grandma!" and "To hell with Bourdette." A real circus.

Not even the hunters came to her defense. How could they? She'd broken every rule of the sport. A few went on television to explain the art of tracking one deer for days. Others invoked professional ethics and the importance of understanding cervine anatomy in order to spare your prey as much suffering as possible.

The whole thing made me sick. Those young folks who were so scandalized are the same ones who come to the benefit receptions at the museum, the ones who let their offspring rummage through the drawers in the gift shop and play hide-and-seek behind the sculptures on the ground floor. While their parents, armed with canapés and glasses of champagne, save the world from genetically modified produce and stop the deforestation of the Amazon basin, their sticky little hands slide over century-old crystal lamps, stain the curtains, leave smudges all over the Dalí and Rothko reproductions, and steal postcards.

Soon enough, though, they'll start losing three percent of their bodily function every year, too. Soon enough, they'll know what it's like to feel something inside them die every minute of every day. They'll panic. They'll stop worrying about saving the deer and start going to the gym three times a week. They'll start thinking about a vacation in Thailand, fast cars, one-night stands with much younger women or men who don't speak their language. Until all that proves useless, too. Like yoga, or mindfulness. Next come the doctors, nice young men and women usually worried about whales in the South Atlantic, who, without taking their eyes off the chat window on their computer screen, will confirm the grim prognosis: there's nothing left to look forward to. By then, it'll be too late for them to escape their complicated lives by running for the woods. And they'll realize none of it mattered all that much, anyway.

My first deer still had its spots. I killed it with a Marlin 336. And I'd do it again. Matter of fact, it's what we do every weekend.

CRE

Her first night alone in the apartment on Edmond Street, she made sure to turn on the television and one of the lights. She fell asleep on the couch. Morning came, and her mother still wasn't back.

The second night was the same.

So was the third.

For three days, she ate leftover chicken and slept on the couch, not wanting to upset the delicate balance of a life Emma Lynn might return to at any moment. She went to school, trying to act normal and not think. Whenever her doubts crept up on her in the middle of class or a conversation with her classmates, she'd cage them inside a battle cry, a sharp twist of her neck, a tug on her hair. Some of the kids probably saw her bite her arm or mutter a few words into the wind, but she was sure none of them suspected she'd become a left-behind.

The dropouts abandoned their children in public places, sometimes without warning; sometimes they planned it out. It was part of the call. It was happening less and less, but it still happened. They left the children in front of churches or schools. Or, more often, in front of city hall. They never considered leaving their children with relatives; that would undermine the gesture. Part of the idea was that they were rejecting the duty of parenthood and returning the children to their rightful guardians. Mothers and fathers were going on strike. They cursed the day they had agreed to participate in this crumbling society by bringing more people into it, and hoped that their withdrawal would overwhelm its institutions, speeding its collapse.

But that day never came. The government found ways to deal with the left-behinds. At first, they sent them to orphanages, but people started to complain that the regular orphans were being mixed in with the children of those maniacs. A special shelter was set up for them. Farms and factories, too, so the older ones could be used for manual labor. This may have taken a toll on the opposition; it showed them that the system had a thousand and one strategies for turning their protests into production. Their numbers dwindled and they kept to the margins. They began to celebrate social invisibility as a form of resistance, though they sometimes intervened in the urban landscape with art designed to wake the city from its "deadly capitalist dream." Rumor had it that only the original group remained, ten or twelve people at most. It was easy for them to avoid the police, who were busy dealing with the everyday crimes of a city where unemployment was on the rise and one in every three homes stood empty.

Government statistics showed a decline in the number of left-behinds, but a few sensational cases still made it into the papers, mostly because the dropouts had lost their revolutionary sheen and everyone now saw them as a misguided sect led by a Finnish mystic and a graffiti artist who refused to give up the lies of the sixties. One especially famous case was a boy left in a little wooden boat with a sign that said: "History does not repeat itself." The child—not a baby at all, but a chubby kid around seven years old—was ceremoniously adopted by the mayor's family in an attempt to usher in a time of reconciliation between society and those who had gone on strike.

At least her mother hadn't done anything as dramatic as that, or left her in a public place like Jimmy B.'s father, who tied him to the statue of Förster. Berenice knew all too well what would happen if anyone figured out she was a left-behind. The image of Jimmy B. standing in a corner of the gym with paint all over his face, glue and colorful tempera paint running down his shirtless back, was enough to convince her that she needed a plan.

At noon on the fourth day, she managed to find one last hope that had survived her earlier fears: her mother must have gone to visit Dorotea, that friend she talked about all the time. Dorotea lived in Guatemala and was very, very rich. Berenice imagined her sitting on stacks of money in the shade of a palm tree. She and Emma Lynn had gone to school together a long time ago. It was hard to visit her, though, because she was always traveling. It was more likely that her mother had gone to visit the man with the carnation. Berenice could have called him "the man from the museum," since that's where she first saw him, but then he showed up at the auction not long after that and bought the *Gloria artificialis*, so she associated him more with the flower. He was tall and thin with white hair. He'd been calling the store nonstop ever since. And her mother had gotten at least two postcards beginning "Dear Celeste," followed by one or two lines of "please" and "still holding on to hope." Maybe she'd decided to go see him after all. But if she had, why wasn't she back yet? No, she'd probably gone to visit one of her friends.

But when Berenice reached the top of the stairs, she remembered that all of her mother's clothing—even her yellow dress—was still in the closet by the front door. As hard as it was to admit, deep down she knew Emma Lynn Brown would never have gone on vacation without her lucky dress, or abandon the plants in her shop. She wasn't there, either; Berenice had checked on the first day. She'd gone over that first afternoon, certain that her mother was just working late on some experiment. But all she'd found was the dark order of the flowers.

The wrinkle creams were all still lined up on the bathroom

shelf, too. Emma had spent nearly half of what she'd made off a commission from city hall on those little magic jars. She'd lined them up according to use: first, the under-eye serum, a must for every woman who didn't want to hit forty looking like a used dishrag, and then the day cream, which worked best in the morning but left Emma's face sticky and shiny for a while, like she'd rubbed it with lard. Last came the night cream, the strongest of the three, which women who were too old to have children needed to apply with special care because they'd gone to a place of no return, a zone some people called the golden years and others just old age, and which Emma called the land of the walking dead.

The first thing Berenice did when she got back to the apartment that Thursday was lower the blinds: she had to take inventory and didn't want the neighbors to know. Especially not Mr. Müller, who could show up at any moment asking about her mother. She stood on a chair and started pulling the cans and jars from the cupboards and setting them on the kitchen counter. According to her calculations, she had enough food to last her several months. At least through the winter. She found some money under the mattress of the pullout couch where her mother slept, along with a gold ring she'd never seen before. Emma kept her jewelry in a heart-shaped box, and Berenice had always helped her pick what looked best with the dress she was wearing. She was sure her mother had never worn that ring, a thin gold band with a sad little diamond straining up from it. She sat there for a long time, turning it over between her fingers. This, she could live on for a while.

As quick as the thought, her hand closed in shame around the ring and made it disappear behind her back. Hysterical laughter bubbled up from deep in her belly and Berenice cackled, with closed fists and dry eyes, rolling from side to side on sheets that smelled of hair spray.

Another important part of the plan was to keep talking. No one would believe that an apartment like theirs, where the banging of pots and pans normally competed with shouting matches and running feet, would suddenly fall silent. Berenice stopped laughing; she wrapped the ring in a red handkerchief and put it back under the mattress. She stood there with her hands on her hips and her eyes on the place her body had just occupied, and began to scold herself in a deep, angry voice. She made sure to call herself a "degenerate" and a "little whore," "degenerate" and "whore" being two words she'd needed to look up in the dictionary that afternoon Emma caught her playing her water game.

If it had been the summer, she could have gone outside right then to play it. No one was there to stop her. She could have let the hose tangle around her like a boa constrictor, and soaked herself from head to toe in the sweeping cascade that watered the little yard behind their apartment. She'd recently discovered how good the spray felt between her legs and had started aiming it there, holding it so close the water would hit her like a hard, sweet hand, and Berenice would fill that hollow with laughter and twistings that almost managed to propel her out of her body, out of her story, out of the world. Until Emma told her she wasn't allowed.

Berenice believed in water. Her idea of heaven was a tumble of waves and foam. But instead of dreaming of a lake or a house by the sea, she dreamt of a flood that would transform the city into an aquatic labyrinth that people would have to navigate in canoes and steamboats. Or, better yet, a city where everyone lived on boats. A houseboat was definitely her ideal home. It didn't even have to be big: the sumptuous movement of the waves would be enough to make it seem like a palace. The rain, bath time, and the water game were substitutes that held her over until that magnificent moment arrived, and whenever things didn't turn out the way she wanted, she opted for one of those forms of happiness. But it was already fall—a cold one, at that; she didn't feel like a bath, and Celeste had been missing for four days.

Her mother hated it when Berenice called her Celeste. She said no one was allowed to use that name. Not even the man with the carnation.

"Dear Celeste!" Berenice shouted in the empty apartment, "Dear Celeste!" as she ran toward the closet, where she buried her face in her mother's dresses and coats. "Dear Celeste!" Gloves and shoes, balled-up socks and shawls went flying, even the old fur coat with its mothball smell. She even tossed a few silk scarves high in the air, where they writhed briefly, like melancholy streamers. "Celesssssste!" she yelled with the little bit of breath she had left, and raced across the room. She reached the safety of a nook behind the chest of drawers just moments before the imaginary hand closed around one of her braids.

The laughter returned with her triumphant escape. And in that dark corner, hugging her drool-damp knees, Berenice fell asleep.

She woke up almost immediately. A shaft of afternoon sunlight was coming in through the window. She'd only been asleep for a few minutes, but she had trouble returning to the present of her plan. If it had been up to her, she would have turned on the TV and forgotten about the whole thing. But there was no time to waste if she didn't want to end up like Jimmy B. Anyway, there was nothing good on at that hour.

She left the apartment, careful not to be seen. She decided not to try the cemetery. She didn't want to use up her limited resources in one day. The cemetery wasn't as easy as the survival game, where you had to go a whole week without spending the five-dollar bill you had in your pocket. She had to overcome all sorts of tests and temptations (the bakery, the ice cream shop, the candy store) before the bill met its destiny in something new, not those old crutches of chocolate and sugar. The cemetery was like the water game: you had to save it for when things got really bad. And with the sun falling soft between the treetops as she walked along the avenue, wrapped up in her green coat, things didn't seem so bad.

The only thing Berenice really needed was a relative who would show up at the apartment every so often and say they were taking care of her while her mother visited her dear friend Dorotea.

A relative was easier to find than a father.

Than a mother.

Than a five-dollar bill.

And the street was full of possibilities.

2

After that first defeat—the undetected disappearance of the bread—he kept his eyes glued to his phone for the rest of the morning. He made sure to check it at regular intervals, except after lunch, when Miss Beryl stuck her head in to ask if he'd finally taken a look at the third-floor displays. Of course he hadn't. The third floor—as Miss Beryl knew perfectly well—was out of his jurisdiction. And hers, too: her only function at the museum was to be in charge of the ticket counter and the gift shop. Vik would've liked to remind her of this. But Miss Beryl had been there forever and enjoyed certain privileges and a level of respect he simply couldn't fathom. She didn't work on weekends and had more vacation days than any other employee. Not only that, but the directors consulted her when they had to make important decisions. When they decided to connect the two buildings—so a single ticket would provide admission to both the Art Museum and the Museum of Natural History—not only had she attended the meeting, she'd also had the charming idea of sticking the life-sized statue of a *Diplodocus* in the plaza next to the main entrance. The dinosaur had been a huge success with children and tourists alike, a fact that Miss Beryl never missed an opportunity to repeat to anyone who would listen.

A few museum employees said that the old lady belonged to the branch of the Family that had fallen on hard times. That's why the city couldn't fire her: she'd been inherited along with the artworks and copies of classical sculptures (which Vik found repulsive) on display in the lobby. It had all been accumulated in the shadow of the steel factory—just like the acid rain, the public library, one or two financial scandals, and plenty of good intentions.

Vik didn't see giving someone a lifetime position at the ticket counter of a museum as such a grand gesture. Miss Beryl's office was perfectly located for her to monitor everything that happened in the lobby, and no one went in or out of the museum without her knowing. She could even see Vik come in every morning through the side door. One day she'd work up the courage to corner him, he thought; she'd block his path on his way to the lift and finally toss out that question, the one that combined compassion and disdain for a man still in the prime of his life who insisted on wearing "ethnic clothes," speaking with a British accent, and walking with a cane.

But that moment never came. For now, the old lady contented herself by interrupting him with a different excuse every day. It could be a glove left behind on one of the wooden benches, a suspicious package, or a crack in the neck of a zebra that (Miss Beryl knew perfectly well) had been there since the museum opened. This time it was the scenes in the Hall of Man. No one had paid them any attention for months— especially not since Smithfield had been hospitalized—and Miss Beryl insisted there were repairs that needed to be made.

Deep down, Vik was glad to be distracted from the video feed. But he feigned displeasure anyway. He tossed a rag onto his worktable (partially hiding his phone), rummaged around in a drawer for Smithfield's keys, removed his smock, and followed the old lady to the lift. Two things heightened his annoyance: he noticed that Miss Beryl had adopted an exaggeratedly sluggish pace (which only made things worse: everyone knows that canes work best when the person using them takes long, quick steps), and that she was wearing the same clothes as the day before (meaning she'd just spent seventy-two hours in the same tracksuit). Vik always wondered how the directors didn't notice these things. Not only had Miss Beryl no sense of proper attire, she always managed to look like she'd just rolled out of bed. Even those curls, which must have required some kind of upkeep, seemed like a wig set badly on her head. Luckily, the lift was full of visitors, which at least spared him thirty-five seconds of discomfort.

The Hall of Man was the least popular area of the museum. The first thing you saw was the shadowy ice of the Unamoi, followed by the little adobe homes of the Comalli, and finally the mountains of the Primevals. In what seemed less like a didactic strategy than an attempt to frighten the public, Smithfield had insisted on low lighting. The mannequins suddenly appeared after one passed through narrow pathways and typical dwellings that had been re-created in meticulous detail. In one stretch, the visitor would crawl through an Unamoi ice tunnel and practically fall into the lap of a Comalli woman milling cornmeal in her hut while singing the same melody over and over. Her daughter was getting married in the next scene. At least, that's what Vik had always thought, because Smithfield had given the two mannequins many of the same features. Finally, at the end of a stone path gradually overtaken by vegetation, the visitor reached the woods of the Primevals. Scattered around were display cases with the few autochthonous pieces in the museum's collection: arrowheads, embroidered textiles, a few baubles and ceramic cups.

Vik had learned a lot from Smithfield, though their talents differed widely. He was in charge of the animals, Smithfield of historical dioramas. He could duplicate any scene taken from a book or a sketch, down to the last detail. His obsession with minutiae, lighting, and sound effects had won him the respect of his colleagues and several historians. Despite the controversy surrounding his ideas about such representations, Vik thought the scene of the Primevals was his best work. It was astonishing how—on the basis of a few letters, a poem written on deer hide, and a sketch made by a sixteenth-century traveler—Smithfield had been able to resurrect a lost people.

Miss Beryl pointed to the Comalli bride behind the glass. At first, all Vik could see were the girl's enormous eyes, which seemed all too aware of the fate that awaited her in the harsh features of her future mother-in-law. These were exactly the same as her betrothed's. Vik had always wondered if Smithfield had played up the similarity intentionally or if it had just been a question of budgetary restrictions, because the mother and son had exactly the same face and it was impossible to be certain which of them would be taking the girl to bed at the end of the celebration. No wonder her mother had stayed home milling corn instead of attending the wedding. Behind the three main players, someone—most likely the best man— was approaching with a recently sacrificed piglet slung over his shoulder. The animal's blood ran down his shirt; one or two drops had fallen next to his sandal. The bride in her short cotton dress, surrounded by her new family and frozen forever in the act of holding out a tray with an ear of corn, seemed to be imploring something of the viewer. A child, two dogs, a musician, and an amiable pig that looked nearly alive (courtesy of

Vik) completed the bridal party, which occupied no more than forty square feet. Smithfield had insisted that every one of the characters was essential. The combination of traditional and modern elements, which spoke to the lives of the Comalli on the reserves, had been celebrated by the museum's administration. Vik always wondered how a real Comalli would feel if they were to visit the exhibition, though that wasn't very likely.

"There." Miss Beryl gestured with her chin as she wiped her nose with a tissue.

Vik looked at the girl's feet. It was true. The gourd full of seeds that had been tied to the best man's free hand was now on the ground next to the bride's left foot and had a crack in it. The cord, which was thin, had probably snapped under the weight. That was the only explanation. It wouldn't be easy to repair the crack in the gourd; it would have to be replaced. Vik doubted that the museum had another piece like it: Smithfield had worked hard on that replica, which was the only evidence of the cultural influence that the Primevals had on the Comalli. In fact, he'd made it by copying rattles that Vik had brought from Coloma.

Explaining that to the old lady—who was still wiping her nose as if she'd just discovered she had one—would have required too much patience. Vik opted for a lie.

"I see," he said, running his fingers through his hair like someone considering an idea for a moment, discarding it, and then settling on a better one. He paused.

"Thank you for letting me know. I'll see to this immediately." And, punctuating the adverb with a tap of his cane on the glass, he turned and walked to the lift as quickly as he could.

Of course he wasn't planning to do anything of the sort.

He dismissed the matter as soon as he was back in front of the moth-eaten snake. The problem was that he also forgot about his phone.

He worked nonstop all afternoon, absorbed by the image of Smithfield on the day of his attack. More than a week had gone by, but hardly anyone was talking about it. Then again, what else could you expect from guides who came and went and had learned everything they knew about the museum from a manual and an hour-long video? If anyone there could compete with Miss Beryl in seniority, it was Smithfield. Not only did he know the museum well, he was the only one who could make the old lady shut up with a glance. Vik still remembered the afternoon when Smithfield had interviewed him for a position in the workshop. He'd always known that his interest in the Ploucquets (and not his limited experience in a museum in Coloma) had won him the job and, eventually, the trust of his supervisor. Smithfield's worktable on the other side of the room—completely covered with materials, toolboxes, notebooks, and paint jars—seemed like a kind of reproach. Vik still hadn't gone to visit him in the hospital. He had his own problems, Vik told himself as he set the perfectly restored snake on a wooden tray. Only then did he remember that his life was being dictated by the whims of a stranger, and his cell phone reappeared under a rag and a few tubes of glue.

The screen displayed an image of his kitchen, empty and off-key. He felt like he was looking into someone else's home, or as if a paintbrush laden with grays had been erasing his, day by day. It was ten to five and his back was beginning to hurt. He barely had the strength to think about doing his exercises at the gym. He felt the absurdity of his situation as an intense dizziness. This symptom was completely new, and he needed to brace himself against his table to avoid falling. When he recovered, now wearing his blazer and about to turn out the light, he noticed one or two inexplicable tears sliding down his cheeks.

☞

I got the idea the day Smithfield showed up at my house. We hadn't talked about anything personal in years, but he came to see me a little while after they sentenced Emilia to community service at the zoo. I bet people figured it was just the thing to put us in our place: baking cookies and cakes, going to church every Sunday, lavishing our wisdom on whoever crosses our path, loving our grandchildren more than ourselves, knitting scarves for the whole family.

Watching an old woman push wheelbarrows full of manure restored divine balance in their lives. I even overheard a red-headed couple say Emilia shouldn't be allowed to wear gloves. So the contact with shit could cure her sudden naturephobia. Of course there's no such word, but that's how they diagnosed her. They've got no sense of shame to keep them from award-ing themselves an honorary doctorate in line at the supermar-ket, raising their voices and furrowing their brows while their tattooed hands caress a recently purchased watermelon. And they won't stop there. Not by a long shot. Now that they feel authorized to teach us lessons, they toss out terms and embrace the unexpected pleasure of a neologism that swoops in to save them, to name the unnameable: in this case, the cold-blooded killing of a fawn at the hands of a degenerate old woman.

I have to give her credit: Emilia earned our respect. She went to work in her finest clothes—long evening gowns she hadn't worn in years, diamond necklaces and earrings. As far as I know, she never got any more than the hems dirty. She did everything elegantly, intentionally slow. At least, that's what she said, though I suspect her lumbar arthritis had something to do with it, too. She quickly became the zoo's newest attraction. People showed up first thing in the morning to watch her clean the zebra cage. The hem of her dress would be dragging dead leaves and alfalfa hay behind it, but Emilia just kept sweeping, ignoring it all with her gaze fixed somewhere past the bars of the cage and her hands clasped around the shaft of the broom like she was about to beat the spectators with it. Anyone who didn't want to end up like Bambi knew better than to get too close. Kids placed bets on her. Emilia was so slow that they'd guess how long it would take her to bring the wheelbarrow full of manure from the antelope enclosure (the zoo doesn't have any white-tailed deer, but wouldn't it be ironic if it did?) to the dumpster. They would laugh, their mouths full of Tootsie Rolls, each time the hunched old woman dressed like a queen got stuck in the mud, earning a Guinness World Record in moving animal excrement from point A to point B with astronomical slowness.

As I was saying, Smithfield came to see me a little while after Emilia was sentenced. It was a Sunday morning. He showed up unannounced. He knew perfectly well he'd find me at home. What he didn't know was that Sunday mornings are sacred to me. There's something all the old folks who complain about insomnia and muscle pain should know: the body needs training. I'm not talking about the gym. That's for the ones who are trying to stop time. They can keep their delusions made of a little sweat and a lot of Botox. No. The secret is training the body to think it's still alive, tricking it with little diversionary tactics. There are many. Sex is one of the most effective.

So many people are scandalized by the thought of two seniors united in the act of copulation. The same ones who invoke nature and common sense and then contaminate our drinking water with hormones. Soon enough we're all going to have fantastic tits thanks to the birth control pills the purification plants can't seem to filter out. All very natural. But when it comes to old folks, nature's not worth a thing. They imagine that along with menopause and discounts for movies and public transportation we get stuffed with silica gel and have all desire sucked right out of us. "From now on, you'll be a mind only," the doctors repeat like a mantra from under their respectably dyed hair. "Abandon all vagina, ye who enter here. Embrace thy bingo and crosswords, thy childhood memories and television programs, thy off-season cruises and nocturnal emissions."

If it were up to them, we'd all be Barbies and Kens. Dolls without tongues or pleasure buttons, without dicks or redeeming holes. Someone should teach the kids. Make senior dolls, so they can start imagining their future. Ready-to-use pre-mortem toys with wrinkled faces, stiff joints, and—of course—zero right to that little death. She'd come with a skein of yarn and knitting needles, he'd look wise in a hat and little spectacles; both would be drooling with joy, their yearning drowned in dozens of sedatives and no urgent needs that aren't solved by a good case of intimate dryness or fold after fold of flaccid skin. But wait! There's much more action still ahead, brought to you by the foresight of a nice pension. Barbie plays solitaire while Ken sits in the sun with a blanket over his legs and a cat in his lap until he falls asleep and his glasses slide down his nose. In another amusing episode, Barbie sets fire to the house with the help of Dr. Alzheimer, who stalks the couple as ruthlessly as any television villain. Barbie and Ken at the Old-Age Home. The kit comes complete with an overbearing nurse and absentee relatives. "Teach your children today about the incontinence of tomorrow." Fun for the whole family, Beryl Hope guarantees it.

We get old. Fact. But how it happens is the opposite of what most people think. The body sends messages and the brain gets surprised. It hurts when I sit down; when did I bang my knee? Is this a bruise, or did a vein just explode? Could've given me some warning. What's my neighbor's name, again? Is that him in the green car? Or have we never met? The mind gets disoriented, begins to question. Are we losing muscle mass, blood pressure, memory? Are we speaking in tongues? But it's no harder to confuse it in the opposite direction. Wasn't it just yesterday that we kissed that boy in the alley behind the bakery? Of course it was. It felt like sucking on a scoop of ice cream. There were still leaves on the trees, and we were wearing that blue twill dress. If a gal concentrates on sending her brain these opposite kinds of signals, she can convince it she's still alive. It's easy, once you know the tricks. For my Sunday morning diversionary tactics, all I need is my old velvet bolster pillow.

I found it in a secondhand shop. I read somewhere that in China they train little girls with a pillow attached to a wooden board. That's probably the best combination. For years, I was stuck with regular pillows, which are too soft to get the job done. It's like having a skinny, limp hand cupped around you. A tease made of feathers that barely gets you hot for the first five minutes, and then, poof. It doesn't matter how you mount it, the thing always ends up deflated and refusing to participate anywhere past the lips, never delivering a real release "down there," as my mother used to say. Velvet is much more effective: it offers resistance but isn't too hard, and it has a fuzzy, rough texture that feels just like skin.

It's great exercise. Especially for the thighs and forearms.

I never really liked it on my back, personally. Too artificial. Feels like rubbing a magic lantern that never does its bit. Better to move your hips and let friction do its thing. Sometimes I wonder how many other women have used that same pillow. I suspect it was designed specifically for the purpose: it's not too big or too small, not too hard or too soft. It's the perfect size and texture. Must have been made in China. I almost asked the woman at the secondhand shop, but she didn't seem too informed about the thousand and one ways to do without a man.

Of course, when a man participates in the process unknowingly, it can add an unexpected layer of satisfaction to the whole thing. I'm not talking about what people call fantasies. Too obvious and intentional. I'm talking about those strange moments when chance intervenes to drop a cherry on top. That's what happened the Sunday when Smithfield came to see me.

It was around nine. I'd just had breakfast and was back in bed, part of my ritual on my days off. Another good trick is to hold your pee as long as you can. The pressure from your bladder makes for an interesting contraction and you feel like you're all full and expanding down there. That was me, that morning: totally concentrated on my pillow, with my tits in a bra two sizes too small that I'd bought on sale and my underwear pushed a little out of place (never underestimate the secondary effects of tight clothing), when my doorbell rang. I decided to ignore it. It wouldn't have been the first time I went downstairs half naked to be greeted by a pair of Jehovah's Witnesses or some other offer of salvation bought and paid for in unbeatable monthly installments. I squeezed my legs and tried to concentrate on a picture in the magazine I'd left open next to the bed (not usually necessary for me). It was

a *National Geographic*. The photo was of two men in turbans. I
didn't find either of them attractive, but there was something
in their eyes. I imagined it was me and not the photographer
they were staring at with that look of surprise on their faces,
their lips parted and their hands reaching under their tunics
for their dicks. That was when I heard the front door open and
close gently and then a few long, heavy strides, the kind that
carry a real dick with them, not one from a magazine. They
made the wood floors creak and then stopped at the foot of
the staircase. The two men in the photo were moving their
hands more frantically now, their eyes rolled back and their
mouths stretched into vulgar smiles of surrender. I sped up,
too. I squeezed and shook, feeling each of the man's steps as he
climbed the stairs. It would have been impossible to stop, much
less turn back. My mind was swimming in circles of delicious
stupor, lost inside the black hole that my body's movements
had tossed it into. And in that perfect moment, I heard his
voice. Firm, serious, right. He said my name. Three times. Or
maybe I should say that my name left his mouth in time with
the three final spasms down there in my parts, which writhed
in shame and pleasure when they recognized the man they'd
been in love with for so long.

"Berilia." I heard him use my name from another era.
"Berilia," he repeated, not daring to open my bedroom door.
He sounded worried, or angry. Then he returned to an almost
military tone, but there was a sweetness there, still. "We need
to talk, Berilia."

♏

There was Connie, for example. She probably wouldn't turn
down a warm bed. But the problem with her was that everyone knew her. No matter how many baths and new clothes

she was given, anybody could still recognize her as the old lady with the short, spiky hair who pushed a shopping cart full of packages around town. It wasn't going to be easy—Berenice mentally browsed her mother's closet—to transform her into an acceptable member of the family.

Connie was like the picture of Max Cercone hanging in the barbershop on Nguyen Avenue: nobody could have described it, but everyone knew it was there. Early in the morning, when it was time to go to school, she was already rummaging through the dumpsters behind neighborhood restaurants, always in a matching pink slip and leggings, a green army jacket and white sneakers. And red lipstick. Her main activity was shouting at the people who walked past her. Sometimes she would scream long strings of insults, other times she'd let out short, hollow grunts like she was burping words in reverse.

Berenice hadn't even considered the other obstacles, like the fact that Connie's skin was so white it would be almost impossible to pass her off as a relative. She crossed the street with determination and asked the woman if she'd like to come over for tea. Connie stared at her for a long time, making sure that the girl wasn't having a laugh at her expense. She pulled a slow hand from her pocket, grime drawing a map of wrinkles across it, and extended it until the tips of her fingers grazed one of Berenice's braids. She returned the hand to her pocket just as slowly. An entire minute passed before she pursed her lips, squinted, and said, "Okay."

When they reached the apartment, Berenice had to help her climb the stairs. It seemed like her knees hadn't bent in years. After every step she paused, brought her hand to her chest, and breathed heavily through her mouth. Halfway up, she had a moment of doubt. She hunched over as if she'd heard an alarm go off inside her or was listening to a whispered warning. She turned as if she was going to leave, but Berenice hung from her arm with all her weight. The old lady had no other choice but to keep going, amid shouts and unintelligible insults. One neighbor (the Russian in apartment six) opened and closed the peephole of his front door. *Good*, thought Berenice. *This way they'll know I'm not totally alone and nobody will come and take me away to the farm for abandoned children.*

Once they made it inside the apartment, Connie chose the pink couch near the doll corner. Berenice hadn't played with dolls in a long time. She'd been collecting them over the years, rescuing them from the trash, the street, and the front yards of nearby apartment buildings. The first one had been a big pink infant with rolls of hard rubber baby fat cascading down her thighs. She was missing an eye, and Berenice was more drawn to its deep dark hole than she was to the dumb blue one that closed every time the doll moved. She'd found her in an abandoned house where a bunch of men used to get together to smoke. They must have used Baby Moon as an ashtray at some point, because when Berenice shook her, a few butts fell out of her head. Berenice took her home, unaware that she was starting a collection. A few days later, on her way back from school, she found a one-legged Barbie between a car's tire and the curb. Next came Queen, a former redhead who had been submerged in blue paint and was transformed into a monarch who only ate vegetables; Barbie Two, who was missing her head and took sleeping pills as a result; and Amelia, the intrepid aviator who was just a torso now, after being detached forever from the airplane that bore her name.

While Berenice made tea, Connie turned on the television. There was a golf tournament on. In the kitchen, Berenice heard the commentator's explanations punctuated by shouts. It sounded like Connie was cheering touchdowns.

By the time Berenice had the tray with tea and cookies ready, the volume was cranked up so high that the commentator's voice came out distorted. It wasn't until she turned the corner, walking slowly along the hallway so she didn't spill the tea, that she heard the old woman screaming:

"You're going to hell, whore, whore, whore."

Connie had Baby Moon on her lap and was rocking her back and forth to the rhythm of her screams without taking her eyes off the television. When she saw the tray, she set the doll on a chair and threw herself at the cookies. As she chewed one after another, she stared at the floor and began to speak in a voice so quiet that Berenice had to turn off the television in order to hear her.

"Things were good for a while." Connie crossed her legs like an actress being interviewed and laughed through the crumbs. "I had a house with a white picket fence and a husband and a peephole to look out at the world through. The husband wasn't bad. Drove a truck. Handled me and it with the same jealous love and rage. Then came God. Three, two, one, zero: God. Showed up one day right around the corner, like the wolf, like our friends from the neighborhood. What, I'm not a woman? I've got muscles like a man. Look, all of you. Feel them. But nobody cares. The white picket fence and the husband, God. Connie and her little hole, zero. One day I went looking for him but I couldn't find him. I can plow, I can cook, I can take my thirty-nine lashes with the best of 'em. Or was it forty? I kept walking. But first I made five kids. They stayed there. Days and nights I walked. There was a fire on a corner. I didn't speak. I didn't sing. But it was good for Connie. I crossed the river and that's where the sentinels found me, guards of the city. *Flagrum taxillatum* for all. For Connie and her little hole. For Connie and her rock and roll. For Connie and her stench factory. To hell with her, whore, whore, fucking whore, and, and. Martha and Mary cried. Lazarus, too. But it wasn't enough. And Connie looked at them with her eyes but not through the peephole she'd had, she looked at them with eyes like doves and saw how the world that was good and beautiful was actually full of thieves and germs, of epidemics and flus and people who washed their hands all the time."

During the silence that followed, Connie bowed her head and amused herself by staring at one of her nails. Then she stood, ate the last cookie, and squatted so her eyes were level with Berenice's.

"Thank you very much," she said, without blinking. She curtsied, thanked the air, and—with an agility unimaginable a few minutes earlier—sprinted out of the apartment and down the stairs.

Berenice sighed. Finding a relative was going to be a lot harder than she'd thought. Outside, the sun was already a line between the silhouettes of the buildings. She picked up Baby Moon and put her back in her place on the rug with the rest of the dolls.

The baby had always been a problem.

Amelia loved Queen with all her torso. She would drag herself across the room to be with her, propelled by her arms and her intrepid memory. Queen would watch her with inebriated eyes and sit motionless in her chair, not even moving the tip of her toe. Worn out by the journey, Amelia would thrust herself upward one last time, grab the monarch's knees, and bury her head between her slippery breasts. She would be so exhausted that she'd let her arms rest, forgotten, on that hair as hard as intergalactic steel wool. Queen would let her stay there for a while. Then she'd fix her sticky gaze on Amelia and run a finger along the contours of her wound. Sometimes the monarch's entire arm would slip inside that hole, and Amelia would writhe in pleasure, suddenly possessed by the blue hand that moved her.

The Barbies only loved each other, or themselves, which was essentially the same thing. They'd tangle in a twinned embrace: one would mount the other like a pair of tongs while the other, with her unmysterious half smile, would caress her shoulder and absent head. Sometimes Barbie Two would get revenge on her playmate by riding her like a horse. She would spur her on with her stiletto heels or a plastic switch. She would pull her braids, her whole body arching and smiling as the uneven gait of her three-legged mount tossed her around. They would end up laughing in a pile as Queen, who approved of everything, beamed at them from her throne. Amelia, sitting in her lap, would chew on the ends of her hair with a dreamy look in her eyes.

But Baby Moon had no one to love her, and that troubled Berenice, who had tried and failed with each of her dolls. The baby was always left out of the game, her mouth permanently open like the black hole of her eye. Surrounded by her companions, her legs spread wide to support the plump mass of her body, Baby Moon would let her oversized head bobble around on her neck until it finally gave in and her jowls would come crashing down onto her chest, as if she were about to vomit or pray in some vile language. The others couldn't even look at her. They stared at the ground, their heads bowed.

"You're going to hell, whore, whore, whore!" she shouted, trying to imitate Connie while looking directly into the doll's eyes.

Baby Moon didn't say or do anything.

But Queen, Amelia, and the Barbies responded in unison. "Yes! To hell!"

3

Vik woke up on his second day of surveillance brimming with confidence in the plan he'd devised the night before. He couldn't believe that something as simple as not showing up at the museum hadn't occurred to him earlier. Maybe that was why he'd dreamt of beating that man in the Ping-Pong tournament. He'd fallen asleep convinced that his victory depended on just one day of better planning.

After his shower, he performed his morning routine to the letter. He dressed as though he were going to work, read in the kitchen for a while, and left the house at the same time as always. The girl in the café was a bit surprised when he asked for a mug instead of his usual paper cup, but she didn't say anything. Vik chose a table near the window. From there he could see the front door of his house and two of the first-floor windows. He pulled a book, a pencil, a notebook, and his cell phone from his bag and sat down to wait for something to happen.

At around eight thirty, the screen showed a white shadow approaching his refrigerator. It looked like a woman in a night-gown. But she was so short and her hair was so long, tangled, and dark that not only could Vik not see her face, it looked like she was entirely covered in hair. The camera captured her back, bent over in the light of the refrigerator, from which she finally emerged with an apple and a bottle of milk. The woman's calm movements around his kitchen horrified him. He watched her walk over to the sink and carefully wash the fruit, then stretch an arm out toward the cupboard, take out a glass, and serve herself some milk. Then she disappeared. She was probably sitting at the table, but she'd chosen the corner that was out of the camera's range. Vik knew he had only a few minutes to act. But nothing had prepared him for this. He'd considered dozens of possibilities, but none of them involved the intruder being a woman he'd apparently been living with for days. As soon as the lightning bolt of this discovery threw light on the events of the past week, he felt his heart begin to race. His hands clenched in two impotent fists. He had to stand up and fill a glass with water, which he drank in practically one gulp while the café's owner looked on, confused. When he returned to his table, he examined the screen for a while before discovering part of a foot resting on one of his kitchen chairs. The woman had not left her post. But she would, before long. If there was any logic to what was happening—Vik reasoned, a bit surprised by his ability to do so—her next stop would be the loo.

The simplicity of this prediction calmed him a bit. He switched the image to the camera on the second floor, which showed the top of the staircase and the doors to the bathroom, on one side, and to his bedroom, half open on the other. Around ten minutes later, the woman appeared on the steps. He could see only the crown of her head and one of her shoulders. She seemed like a dwarf, but maybe that was just the angle of the shot. Vik estimated she was probably just under five feet tall, since her head barely made it half-way past the third shelf of the bookcase he'd placed on the landing. Then she did something unexpected: she took a few steps back, sprinted through the doorway to his bedroom, and jumped straight into his bed. Vik had to piece this all together from the end of her dash: the camera trained on the half-open door of his bedroom captured the woman's short, round legs rolling around on the bed he'd meticulously made before leaving the house.

The image of this hairy creature rubbing itself on his sheets was more than Vik could bear. He packed his phone and the rest of his things in his bag, then crossed the street as quickly as he was able. He managed to turn the key in the lock without making a sound, but the front door's hinges betrayed him. Vik heard short, quick steps on the floor above him, a small tumult, and then the sound of a door—obviously the one to the hall closet near his bedroom, where he kept blankets that were too heavy for the season, old clothing, and other unused items—slamming shut.

He climbed the stairs calmly, calculating the weight of his foot on each step. Standing in front of the closet, which was actually more like another room, he realized that it had been weeks, if not months, since the last time he'd opened that door. He pressed his ear to the wood and it shot back a cackle. At that point, several things happened almost simultaneously. Vik remembered that his adversary in the dream the night before had an enormous sweat stain on his shirt, a stain that turned sticky and black when the man lost the match, as if he were sweating lava or tar, or something worse. Right then, Vik lost his balance. His legs gave out and he dropped the cane that had been supporting his entire body weight, ending up flat on the carpet with his legs still bent and his arms outstretched.

He realized that his back hurt too much to straighten it, and the feelings of disgust and triumph, which the woman and the dream produced in him in equal measure, sparked a fit of uncontrollable laughter. He imagined the camera sending images of his twisted body to the phone in the pocket of his blazer.

Giving in to the comfort of the carpet and his laughter, which was beginning to relax his limbs, tendons, and cartilage, Vik realized something else: it wasn't the first time he'd seen the woman with all that hair.

He retraced his daily movements, step by step. He saw himself leaving his house with coffee on his mind; he saw himself climbing the four stairs to the café across the street, paying as little attention as one does when passing a local church or a laundromat; he saw himself opening the door and stepping into that smell of chocolate and vanilla and, in that instant, he registered (apparently not for the first time, though it seemed as if it were) a heap bundled in a blanket the same color as the wall, a heap with long black hair that had been there for who knew how long, crouching beside the four steps to the café's front door like the crack in the window of that abandoned church or the faded letters of the laundromat's sign. Vik tried to remember exactly when she'd appeared. No, it hadn't been long ago. Not during the summer, at least. Maybe she'd arrived with the first autumn chill, a few weeks earlier. But when had she abandoned her post by the stairs and sneaked into his house? Impossible to say. If he could barely remember having seen her at some point, how could he have registered her absence from the tiny world of his quarter-to-eight coffee?

It might have been different for someone else (one of those people who find any connection between the new and the old, no matter how flimsy, to have a calming effect), but the thought of that same heap breathing the moth-eaten air of his closet at that very moment didn't calm Vik in the least. Quite the contrary. He stopped laughing, dragged himself over to his cane, and, using the wall, managed to get himself seated upright in front of the closet door.

Yanking the door open and confronting the woman was out of the question. Though the camera showed her in a white nightgown, floating through his kitchen like a jellyfish, Vik imagined her naked. He was ashamed of the thought, but he returned to it again and again. He saw her huddled on a bottom shelf in the closet, her skin covered with hair or dirt, one hand under her head and the other between her legs, the air passing over her wet lips as she breathed in and out in a long spasm, her breasts rising and falling in a tangle of black hair. Wouldn't it be better to bang on the door, or to yell for her to come out on her own? Give her the chance to pull herself together, to rejoin the world? One had to admit that sneaking into a stranger's house and occupying their closet required a certain degree of mental instability. Vik knew of a kind of bird that, by some evolutionary failure, never learned to build nests and went through life displacing those that could, after eating or destroying their offspring. And then there were others that would simply lay their eggs in the first nest they found, leaving their young to be raised by adoptive parents. What kind of disorder could drive a person to those extremes? He imagined the woman sitting next to the café steps, indistinguishable from her blanket, lying in wait day after day for the right moment, maybe the morning when the neighbor's cat had run between his cane and the doorstep and he'd struggled for a few seconds to keep his balance, slamming the door shut without checking the knob. It wouldn't have been the first time he left without locking up; every day, dozens of mishaps interrupted the mechanical actions meant to keep him safe in a city that wasn't his. That event couldn't have gone unnoticed by someone used to watching his every move. No, the woman had not earned his courtesy. Why should he knock on the door of his own closet in a farce of social graces when she'd been the one staking him out? She'd probably heard him laughing like a madman moments earlier, just as she'd probably seen him picking at his toenails or struggling for hours, armed with a pair of tweezers and a mirror, with the hairs peeking out from his nostrils.

He was about to stand up and open the closet door when he found a new reason not to. If, as all signs seemed to indicate, she was the woman from outside the café, who knew what plagues she might be carrying after years living in the street? Vik's arms and legs began to itch at the thought that her favorite pastime seemed to be rolling around on his bed. Again he saw her naked body, which got dirtier every time, plunging under his sheets, kicking with arms outstretched as if she were swimming on his mattress, her hair stuck to her skin like seaweed.

This time, he didn't feel shame at the image of the woman in his bed. It was his body's reaction that made him feel older and sicker. Reaching out to open the door seemed like the most onerous task in the world. Maybe it was better to wait until she needed to leave the closet. She would have to, eventually. Ignoring his erection and the pain in his back, Vik steadied his cane on the floor and stood all the way up.

That was when he remembered he'd forgotten to call the museum. But it was Saturday, no one would really notice his absence. He was glad that at least one of his problems was so easily solved.

⌃

The last time he called me Berilia we were still the picture of strength and health, the deer population was still under control, and people still believed in the atomic bomb and household appliances. Back then, changing our names had seemed romantic. It reminded us of outlaws in black and white, the night sky stretching over a dark and dangerous couple as they headed for the Wild West or the lawless expanses of silver-screen Mexico, two people on the run who maybe, for a moment, we resembled.

Smithfield didn't bring any of that up, that morning. He was right not to: if he'd insisted on talking about Gabi like he had so many times before, I'd have thrown him out. But the last thing I expected as he sat comfortably at my kitchen table, and I distracted myself with the coffee and my badly tied robe, was for him to start talking about our role as senior citizens in a city that either ignored us or attacked us without even trying to sugarcoat it.

He talked about Emilia, about the injustice of the campaign that had been launched against her. And the hostility that the whole thing had sparked in the younger generations. Another symptom of an imbalance in the social body, he said. I didn't like that he was describing something that was actually pretty normal like it was some kind of medical pathology. Since when did youth respect what their elders did? We certainly hadn't, I reminded him. And anyway, what's all this about a "social body"? Nothing gives us the right to think we're part of something bigger than ourselves, much less a body. It's a deceptive analogy. I learned something a long time ago: if you manage to save yourself, you do it alone. He sounded like one of those awful news shows, the kind that go on about the apocalypse and suggest group outings with bats and torches. And I told him so.

"Fine. But we can't stand around with our hands on our hips while they push us aside," he said, taking the last sip of the terrible coffee I'd served him (that was Frank: it didn't matter if the situation wasn't ideal, he'd drink it down anyway, to the last drop).

It was already hard to follow what he was saying that morning. At some point he jumped from the "social body" to nature, which also showed clear signs of an imbalance. He talked about the deer, about their unprecedented violence over the summer. He suspected that something in the woods was driving them mad. He cited a few medieval etchings or illustrations that showed them eating meat. Snakes. And the entrails of hares and other mammals. I told him that it wasn't so unusual. That in Scotland they'd found a bunch of decapitated birds with no wings or legs, but with their bodies perfectly intact. The biologists studying the phenomenon had been bewildered (what kind of predator eats the worst parts of the prey?) until they discovered that the culprits were local deer. Seems like because of us—or because of the Scots, at least— the weeds that provide the minerals deer need for their antlers to grow had disappeared from the forest, and their instinct for self-preservation had taken over: the deer went down to the coast and ate dozens of pigeons and petrels—choosing the parts of the birds that contained the most calcium, and in the process exhibiting a wisdom few of us could ever hope to achieve.

Frank looked at me as if what I'd just said was the stupidest, most obvious thing he'd ever heard. He replied that he'd been talking about something else, about cultural symbols like the serpent-devouring stag. Which had nothing to do with that traditional idea about priests swallowing the sins of men but remaining as pure as the animal. That was a load of religious garbage. But it was also one of the early cultural signs of the final imbalance, of how the entire planet would eventually rise up against us. A bunch of Jung and the shadow. A bunch of years spent sad and lonely, I'd say. Then he reminded me that we'd seen a deer acting strangely back at Bridgend. True. But it had been Gabi's deer, so I didn't say anything. I didn't want to give him the chance to talk about any of that. I preferred to let him "enlighten" me. Frank always did have a didactic streak; it had been one of his charms.

Not anymore. If he's got a streak now, it's a losing one. Nothing's left of that tone of his, and all that knowledge, but the casing—just an old man with chafed skin lying in a hospital bed. If he's lucky, some nurse might grope him a little now and then. There are people who talk to the comatose in the hope that some part of their brain can still hear. I've heard about parents who hooked their daughter up to a stereo playing her favorite album on repeat. And then there was the wife who got tired of praying, so she plugged her husband into one with religious chants. That way, all she had to do to improve his chances of recovery was pick up the phone and tell the nurse to press Play. Imagine if those patients really could hear. It would be hell. Fact: you'll never find me sitting at anyone's bedside, much less connected to some machine.

That Sunday, I decided to let Frank do the talking. I couldn't have cared less about his theories of imbalances, symbolism, and signs. The deer had outnumbered us for a while already, and it just made sense to do something about it. But I hung on his every word, anyway. Not because of what he was saying, but because for the first time in years it seemed as if he needed me, and I was flattered. When he finished, I said to him, half joking, that if the deer were going crazy, the logical thing would be to hunt them. He didn't accept the idea right away: as usual, he wanted to get to the root of the issue, to understand the reason behind the animals' behavior. But I convinced him we didn't have the resources for that. What could a bunch of old folks do in the face of something like this?

In the end, he agreed. He said it would give us a chance to show the rest of the world we still knew what was what, and that having a purpose would make us stronger as a group. Matter of fact, he was the one who suggested I teach the seniors at the community center to hunt. Just picture it, a bunch of rookies in their seventies and eighties! But he didn't say that part right away. First, he took me to the zoo.

There was Emilia, sitting in one of the gazebos with a cup of coffee in front of her. Against the grays, greens, and browns of the cages, her orange dress looked like a scream. Smithfield pulled out a chair. It took me a few seconds to realize that it was for me. Emilia looked up at us without seeing us.

"That woman's been drugged," I said immediately.

"This was what I wanted you to see. It's all any of us will have left before long: clonazepam heaven," he replied in the voice, somewhere between didactic and paternal, that he always used with that handicapped assistant of his. It bothered me a little, and I wondered if I'd given in too quickly to his ideas, if I'd let myself get carried away in a moment of auto-erotic weakness. But I didn't say anything.

"I haven't been drugged. I'm at peace," Emilia interrupted, as if someone had pushed a button.

I wanted to slap her awake. To top it off, she smiled, and her teeth were perfect. Apparently, her pension was better than the benefits we got at the museum.

"Emilia, what they've done to you is bad." Now he was talking to her as if she didn't have a master's degree in French, one husband six feet under, two exes in Florida, and a passport full of stamps.

"Of course it's bad. But it feels good."

"You see?" His eyes (their color was like no one else's, brown with yellow flecks) bored into mine a little too intensely. But I didn't look away. "Berilia, if we don't do something, most of us are going to end up like that soon."

"Us who?" I couldn't tell if he was talking about all of humanity or just Barbie and Ken at the Old Age Home.

What he said next didn't really clear things up. It nudged the catastrophe toward the global, with special emphasis on the hopes that hung on us active seniors. Performing a concrete service for our community would return us to the glory of our youth. Or something like that.

"All of us," he continued. "I'm going to tell you a story."

Where had this man come from, with his chivalry and his pointer finger raised in the air? His lankiness and his height had gotten more pronounced over the years, but what had made him seem hopelessly clumsy in his youth now gave him a knotty, conceptual appeal. Over the course of that morning and several later episodes, I concluded that Smithfield was also being visited by Dr. Alzheimer. That Sunday, though, my lady parts were happy and satisfied and thinking for both of us with admirable lucidity. What a relief it was to let them follow the explanations he gave in his blue blazer and khaki pants with one or two splotches of glue on them. They humored the string of incoherencies coming out of that man, who at least still had all his hair and his boyish smile.

Too bad Frank chose intellectual work. He would've made a fortune off the image of solidity he projected, even as his brain was turning into a sponge. Circuits I didn't even know I had started working again down there. I could feel little currents of electricity I thought had run out a long time ago as he went on about signs and predictions, and we circled the aviary more times than we needed.

I really did try to follow the trail of his ideas. I think deep down I didn't want to believe he'd only started calling me Berilia again because he'd lost all sense of time and his neurotransmitters were disturbed enough that I could be his friend again. But if, for once, a visit from Dr. Alzheimer didn't mean offensive rearrangements of memories and relatives, pouting, uncomfortable silences, and conciliatory pats on the shoulder ("He doesn't mean it, sweetie," or "It's just the disease talking," or "Maybe she'll recognize you tomorrow"), well, I certainly wasn't going to get in the way.

Some people might characterize my attitude as criminal. It's common knowledge that taking advantage of the elderly is illegal in most countries. But if dementia had suddenly erased all those years of guilt and resentment, and Smithfield really believed that nothing terrible had ever happened between us, I'd be the first to embrace Dr. Alzheimer's cause.

The irony doesn't escape me that it was our first date in more than forty years. We even bought and ate some animal crackers. Meanwhile, Smithfield was talking about senior citizens, deer, and the destruction of our planet. It wasn't until he mentioned the Primevals that I began to suspect things weren't all going to be rosy.

I already knew about Smithfield's obsession. The one that had driven him to leave Bridgend, finish college, and travel in search of evidence until the world (in this case, three history PhDs who held chairs at a few universities) accepted the possibility that Smithfield, with no doctorate or reliable mental and physical health, had discovered a previously unknown tribe from the Caribbean that had reached our shores and mixed with the only ancestors we'd thought we had.

I'd followed the story in silence—my default for everything that involved him. His theory had gained traction for a few years. More than anything because it contradicted what we'd been taught about the founding fathers. Especially Förster, who had requested that a brigade of women be immediately assembled to seduce the settlers and make healthy new children because behind us there was nothing, just miles of empty land and forests waiting to be conquered. Now Smithfield was telling us that none of it was true. That the mystery of the Primevals could be our mystery, too. That maybe we also came, in an indirect but real way, from the animals and the woods, and not just from steamships, credit cards, and oil refineries.

The story of the tribe was published in a few research journals. This was back in the seventies, when it was still relatively easy to believe an account of benevolent ancestors in perfect harmony with a nature we'd lost sight of in the pursuit of comfort. People started to talk about returning to the woods, awakening age-old knowledge that had been lying dormant in our DNA. The Family financed archaeological digs at the outskirts of the city, hoping to uncover remains from this shattered genealogy. They didn't find much, but a few arrowheads and tools were enough to land Smithfield a job at the museum, where he created an entire wing for the Primevals. Until the specialists showed up and started dismantling his theory stone by stone. It turned out that Frank had just one piece of evidence: a history painted on Comalli deer hides that turned out to be much more recent than he'd claimed and which, as he confessed after a long interrogation, he'd bought from an antiques dealer who proved impossible to track down.

The controversy was discussed in academic circles for a while. But the general population refused to accept that the theory of the unknown tribe was a fake. Sects of "new Primevals" sprang up on the other side of the Onlo River; people organized rock concerts and founded nonprofits to finance new digs. Lots of young folks refused to let a few historians turn them into white bread without a trace of mystery, just by asserting the real age of an urn. People rummaged around their attics and showed up at the museum with the strangest objects, demanding that they be included in the exhibit. Others tweaked their family trees, looking for ambiguities that would reveal the drop of blood that would make them darker, braver, fiercer.

Smithfield stopped appearing in public. He gradually became a stale joke in university hallways. The Family stood by him until the end, though. The proof is that the display takes up the entire east wing of the Hall of Man. He insisted on that, even though it contains only two figures. He said that the success of the composition depended on all the excess space. It was important to re-create the world as the Primevals experienced it. As white and wide open as albaria's effect on the mind. As immeasurable as the woods and the mountains in the Northeast. Of course, the plaque changed over the years. Now it just says, The Primevals: Myth or Reality? Which seems to answer the question. That's how things stand. And poor Frank knew it. He knows it now, in his hospital bed. Maybe it's a better place for him than where he was. Always shut away in his workshop, delivering his lectures to his assistant, that poor little guy too big for his britches.

A few museum employees say that Smithfield never stopped collecting evidence and was working on a big book that would finally prove his theory. I imagine the undertaking ended up in Dr. Alzheimer's hands. Now I understand that the tall, elegant man in the zoo that day, who got dates and events mixed up and called me Berilia, probably without even realizing it, wasn't a tortured genius or a visionary. I'm the only one who can see the truth behind the wrinkles, behind the restless face the years gave him. And I don't like it. Because it's a truth full of pain. A pain not even an entire imaginary people was able to stop or even slow down. I've always known the Primevals had only one purpose in Smithfield's life, and that was to help him forget Gabi. Those poor natives didn't have any luck there, either. Even that day at the zoo, in the middle of all his plans and incoherent explanations, it was her name and not mine that sparked a glimmer of lucidity in his eyes.

☙

The next day, her mother's clothes cast new shadows over the apartment from where they lay strewn around the bedroom. She hadn't been able to sleep in her own bed this time, either. She'd gotten into Emma Lynn's, where she could keep an eye on the dolls. They'd never spoken before. Berenice stared at them for a long time, weighing the option of putting them away in a box. She decided not to. She straightened Baby Moon's dress, put her in the middle of the circle, and took a few steps back. The scene was the same as always, but something twisted deep down in her stomach.

As she got dressed for school, Berenice decided she wasn't going to lose hope after what had happened with Connie. The woman was clearly off her rocker. She liked that expression. Emma would use it all the time when she was making fun of the old-fashioned education drilled into her by her grandmother Cecilia, whose daughters held "gimcrack" jobs and dated "milksops," while everyone else was always at least a little off their rocker. Emma had explained to Berenice what the phrase meant, but they didn't use it the way the dictionary said. In the middle of some domestic chore, Berenice might announce that she was getting off her rocker, which meant she was going to stop being a good girl for a few minutes and had permission to scream, jump, and throw things at the wall, that is, to do all sorts of irrational things as long as it was only for a short period of time. Emma did it, too, sometimes, especially when she was frustrated with an experiment in the nursery. With the albaria, she'd needed to run through the hills of the cemetery barefoot, smash two or three flowerpots on the ground, and kick over their folding screen, until a single seed was intimidated enough to sprout in the land of the dead.

That was months ago. Emma Lynn had been obsessed with the seeds ever since she found them. Maybe because they were the only living thing that had belonged to Gabi. Berenice could tell that, more than success with some experiment, Emma was looking for her mother in that plant. That's why she was so stubborn about the albaria. She'd tried countless techniques, but none of them worked: tapping and moistening that were meant to reproduce the humid conditions the plant supposedly came from; different kinds of soil and fertilizer. Nothing. She even sacrificed a few seeds to a process of double fertilization that ultimately didn't take.

One afternoon, frustrated and pretty far off her rocker, Emma Lynn had run out of the nursery and straight for the cemetery. It was still cold, but she was barefoot and wore a green-and-white dress that skimmed her heels. Berenice followed her and the two ran without stopping until they reached Great-grandma Cecilia's grave, where Emma Lynn opened her hand and threw the seeds she'd been carrying at the headstone.

A while later, after spring had arrived and the two of them

had forgotten about the whole thing, they discovered a shoot of albaria growing among some rocks pretty far from where they'd thrown the seeds. Emma Lynn had recognized it by the smell its leaves gave off and by their color, a waxy blue over green. She left Berenice to guard the plant while she went back to the nursery for the tools she'd need to transplant it into a flowerpot. She needed to know its secret. And she could only do that by studying the plant, an undertaking she dedicated the entire summer to, and which also ended in failure.

Berenice, on the other hand, had a theory. She believed that the plant had grown there simply because it preferred the land of the dead.

"It's not a magical plant for nothing," she concluded.

The only thing Emma Lynn had told Berenice about albaria was the same thing her grandmother Cecilia had said: that the flower had driven too many people crazy, including Emma Lynn's mother, Gabi Alicia Brown. It was best to stay away from it altogether.

"Everyone has the right to a minute of madness," Emma Lynn had said one day that summer, as she stroked the white and seemingly inoffensive flowers of her first and only albaria.

"But not to four days in a row." Berenice sighed, sitting at the kitchen table and making a list of people who might be able to pass for her relatives.

The ideal candidate was someone who wasn't completely off their rocker, but who wasn't completely on it, either. She immediately dismissed anyone who had children. They probably didn't want another, and the kids wouldn't have room in their lives to go around acting like cousins or big siblings. That eliminated her extended family—distant aunts and uncles Emma had no contact with and who were always making babies, as if they secretly planned to start an army. It was one of the things Berenice was most grateful to her mother for: that she was an only child and had been kept far away from her mass-produced second cousins. No. The only thing she could expect from that part of the family was to be turned over to Social Services.

The issue of progeny also ruled out Mr. and Mrs. Belcher, her neighbors from the building next door. It was a shame because they had two older daughters and a much younger son, Aníbal, who Berenice sometimes played catch with and who didn't get on her nerves too much.

Next to be eliminated were men who lived alone. Emma had warned her about those. If a man was over thirty and was still on his own, there was clearly something wrong with him that made women run screaming. That's why the matchmaking agencies charged them double what younger or divorced men paid. If you were divorced, at least there was a story there; otherwise, you were just suspicious. They can save their mysteries for some desperate chick, Emma Lynn would say. They were clearly not the best candidates for adopting a little girl.

That cut the list down to two categories: women who lived alone, and childless couples who were a little off their rockers. Holding up her pencil, Berenice questioned the air in the kitchen. The best thing would be to start with people who weren't too close to her. Anyone already in her life—her teachers, that old couple on the fourth floor, her classmates' single aunts—would feel obligated to report her to the authorities. The economy of affection would be too much for them. *Sentimentality and shared history are deadweight you need to take into account*, Berenice told herself.

She divided the page into two columns, which she quickly realized was a waste of her organizational skills. When she evaluated each category and adjusted for reality, she discovered that she could think of only one option: Omar and Halley, the owners of Ship of Fools, a café with round windows that was famous across the city for its pumpkin pie.

Berenice had spent many five-dollar bills on the delicacies baked by Halley, a girl with long brown hair who always wore black jeans and T-shirts of the same color. Her left arm was covered in tattoos, but she didn't have a single mark on her right.

"It's because I don't believe in balance or symmetry," she'd told Berenice once, as she served her a green shake. "They're just simplistic lies invented by lazy artists."

On the basis of this philosophy, Omar and Halley had cut different-sized portholes into the walls and roof, which at night made the café look more like a large, luminous spotted animal than a boat.

The Ship of Fools was two blocks from the flower shop and three from the Grandville Avenue entrance to the cemetery. Whenever she got bored helping her mother in the nursery, Berenice would either stroll around the tombstones or go chat with Halley at the café. Berenice did most of the talking, though. Halley would usually respond with a single word, a furrowed brow that nudged her stories forward, or an understanding smile that rounded out their conclusion. Not like Emma, who preferred endless discussions, sermons, and anecdotes.

Omar was tall and thin, too, but his hair was so blond it was almost white. It made Berenice think of farms. He was the one who'd come up with the name of the café, which was part of his personal crusade against the coffee chains that had invaded the city (the whole world, in fact) over the past few years. He spent more time than Halley did at the Ship of Fools, lounging in one of the beat-up chairs in the back, rereading the books piled in a corner next to the board games while the customers wandered wherever they felt like, fondled the cookies and cakes, and, on a few occasions, even poked their heads into the kitchen. Omar didn't care. He claimed this philosophy was behind the success of their venture: no paper cups, no mass-produced goods, no deep cleaning, and no prison-style surveillance. The battle would be won by dint of grime, experimental recipes, furniture and mugs purchased from the Salvation Army or recycled directly from the trash, and absolute freedom of movement.

Students were the first to claim the Ship of Fools as their own. Then came the musicians and the artists, and finally the homeless people from the block; Halley made them packets of cookies from the day before. There were almost never empty tables, especially in winter. With its yellow lights and fogged windows, the café looked like a ship adrift, or maybe a spacecraft ready to abandon a city on the verge of collapse.

That's where Berenice headed that Friday afternoon, after another successful performance at school. She'd been more careful than usual with her homework and her participation over the past few days, and she wondered if maybe she was overdoing it. She didn't want to risk having her teachers feel the need to call Emma Lynn and congratulate her on Berenice's achievements.

"It all comes down to the right balance between telling the truth and lying," she concluded as she walked toward Grandville, wrapped in her green coat and a feeling of hope that, just like the sun at those latitudes, came and went without ever fully shining on her.

4

He called the museum from inside the bedroom, with his eye still on the closet door. Then he went down to the kitchen and pulled from the cupboard every last bottle of soap, bleach, multipurpose cleaner, and disinfectant he could find. He set them on the countertop and looked at them like they were the only rations left after a shipwreck. He hadn't used any of them in months, but just the sight of their labels' promises filled him with a sense of urgency he hadn't felt in years: the kind a person feels when they have a job to do and know they're entirely capable of doing it.

He opened the first-floor windows to air out the smell he hadn't noticed before, but which was clearly there now, clinging to the furniture, the carpets, and the portraits, creeping toward his books, his silver, and his Ploucquet. Penetrating. A smell of earth or leavening. Of decomposition. Of the woman in his closet.

An hour of cleaning interspersed with surveillance of the closet, which he could see from the bottom of the stairs, calmed him down but also completely wore him out. He sat down on the chaise longue he'd bought from an Italian craftsman when he first moved to the city. He barely ever used it; it seemed too beautiful. Now he was certain she'd lain on it. Wasn't it the perfect divan for a damsel in distress? He laughed at the idea of that little body, certainly plagued by odors, being described as belonging to a "damsel." Even when he imagined her on the chaise, it was impossible to picture the woman lying on her back; he still saw her coiled around herself like a contortionist—chin to knees, hands clasped under the soles of her feet, all tucked in under the greasy blanket of her hair. And why not? A homeless woman obviously wasn't going to know that the chaise longue had been a favorite among lovers and courtesans when the hour came to pose for husbands and artists. He was just as certain she'd used it as he was that his entire house had been a stage set she'd wandered through at her leisure, trying on and shedding this thing he called his life.

Vik lifted his feet onto the chaise and reached out to pull a cigarette from the wooden box on one of the three coffee tables in the living room (on the other two sat a magnificently restored Ploucquet and a few nonfiction books that had been popular the year before: *A Biography of Salt*, *The Silk Road*, and *The History of Color*). Vik smoked only occasionally, in his home and only long, slim cigarettes that were getting harder and harder to come by. He didn't understand those people who described themselves as "social smokers," who injected the inconvenience of conversation into the rhythm of their inhalations. Much less the ones who subjected themselves to the cold and to the pity of onlookers during the breaks that "their addiction" imposed. They smoked in groups, hurriedly and wrapped in smiles of complicity, like a gang plotting a robbery they know they're never going to commit.

As was the case with almost everything he did, Vik needed

to concentrate when he smoked. He inhaled at regular intervals. Sometimes he couldn't help counting the seconds (no more than seven or eight) that separated an exhalation from the following pull. His mind slipped into the count on its own and disappeared in the repetition. This withdrawal was part of the enjoyment, abandoning the body to the freedom of the mindless pleasure of circulating air. The same thing happened at work and during any other relatively mechanical activity. He had trained himself at an early age to listen to the rhythms and complaints of his body and eliminate any mental activity that might interrupt them. Prasad was good at it, too, but not as good as Vik, who could reach a state of mental stillness not unlike a Tibetan monk's. Absolute emptiness. Too bad it didn't do anything for the pain. Quite the opposite: the pain only seemed to abate if his mind indulged in delusions of power, if it managed to home in on the unhealthy circuits to which it was fatally connected, and to create—if only for a few seconds—the illusion of absolute control over what was happening. Drugs were better, obviously. Drugs were better than breathing exercises.

He took one, two, three pulls of his cigarette. He was in the third second of an interval when he heard a noise, an impact muffled by something, maybe a throw pillow or some towels. As if someone had dropped a book onto a carpet.

The woman had decided to move.

Vik put out his cigarette, grabbed his cane, and went upstairs. The smell seemed to have returned, or else it had never been gone. There it was. It was the one percent of bacteria that best even the strongest household cleaning products, the stain that becomes an identifying feature of the clothing it clings to. He crouched by the door. Nothing. Then suddenly a noise that, because it was so familiar, he couldn't identify right away. Liquid and plastic. A liquid splashing against a hard plastic surface, probably the sides of a bucket. Disgust returned like a rag shoved down his throat and took the form of the woman urinating into a red bucket (why red? Vik had no idea). Was there anything worse than catching someone as they reached a new level of self-degradation? It even crossed his mind that the act was part of a plan, that the woman was forcing him to tacitly accept her control of a space she'd conquered through humiliation. Very much against his will, he also thought about the opposite: he thought about serial killers, sadists, and torturers who seek precisely that humiliation, that distinct and irreversible regression of the mind that turns the body into a collection of entrails, tissues, and circuits functioning on their own in an unnameable place that has nothing to do with being human.

These inappropriate thoughts (why compare himself to a psychopath or feel responsible for what was happening?) and the image of the woman with the red bucket gave him the courage he needed to open the door. He closed his hand around the doorknob and pulled hard, as if he were about to make a triumphant entrance into a party. The door barely moved: it was locked from inside.

Dozens of alarms went off in his head in the seconds that followed, as he assessed and discarded one hypothesis after another about something bigger than a homeless woman driven to desperation by the early arrival of winter. In a city where so many homes sat empty, no one would choose to risk an occupied one. It must be some kind of plot. Yes, a conspiracy being carried out simultaneously in different neighborhoods across the city. People seizing property and goods, first sending in an intruder and then raising the stakes; people with the time and the patience to plan a devious invasion that ended with the victim giving up the immense, and definitely unten-able, task of defending their "life." People Vik had learned to distrust a long time ago, regardless of the names or classifica-tions attached to them. People with a cause.

Vik had heard about the ones who lived in the woods. Every day they came up with new strategies to educate those who still chose to participate in the "Great Lie." At least, that's what they were calling it in graffiti. "How long will you side with the Great Lie?" written across the mayor's face or a poster for the most famous burger chain in the country, on which they'd also drawn two realistic cockroaches. There was also the one that read "Have you heard? We have" across a land-scape riddled with craters that seemed to allude to nuclear war or some environmental catastrophe.

Vik reproached himself for not having paid more attention to the local news, for not being the slightest bit curious about what was happening in the city where he'd lived for so many years. But he was too fond of showing up at the museum and hearing his coworkers talk about the latest achievements of the little girl who became a professional soprano at the age of twelve or the outrageous price of gas, and blinking at them and smiling back at them like a perfectly detached observer. What happened was that every time the door to his house closed behind him, Vik went back to Coloma. Not to the dev-astated island he'd abandoned, or to the refugee camps, not even to the joy of its rocky beaches. He went back to its words. They were his final stronghold, his impenetrable fortress: the terms he used to grind the indiscreet questions of his cowork-ers to dust, the expressions in which his first times happened over and over again, the language in which his mother was still alive.

It was this language he hurled against the closet door. One, two, three times. He even had enough energy left over to kick the wood, in an attempt that died in midair when one of his tendons objected.

A few seconds later, the woman began to sing.

∽

Because while Smithfield struggles with his neurotransmitters and a machine relieves him of the responsibility of breathing, while my battle against sweets, butter, and gravity rages, Gabi lingers on.

Imagine skin that's dark but luminous, with beauty marks scattered across it (especially the chest); imagine waist-length hair falling thick and dark and curly; imagine brown eyes with a reddish rim like a serpent's, but then erase every trace of malice from them; imagine a face that never needed makeup; an energy, a sound like the sea, a voice to drive you wild. And you still wouldn't be close to imagining the kind of spirit that inhabited those traits or the entity known as Gabi Alicia Brown.

She arrived at the mansion when Smithfield (who was going by Francisco in those days, a name we all thought was much more glamorous) and I had been living there for a few months already, on the second floor with a bunch of students, musicians, and artists. Plus two psychologists: a biochemistry student called Teddy Gutierrez, and Clarke, who always said he was a psychiatrist but looked too young for it. But mostly musicians. Everyone at Bridgend seemed to know how to play an instrument; there were always cases and cables being installed, preparations being made for the Big Concert. The house was teeming with bodies painting, smoking, playing records, eating cheese sandwiches, and lying on the mattresses that covered the floor of the master bedroom.

Some did nothing but think. I was one of them. Thinking

was always my talent. I could sit in the attic for hours, watching a ray of sunlight and opening my mind. Everything fit inside it. I could stretch and contract it at will, like a muscle. It was easy. Especially back then (drugs won't ever be as cheap again, or sex as new and as free). All you needed to do was go to the sessions led by Clarke and Gutierrez and you'd find that door hidden behind the system. All the kids had visions during those experiments. But they weren't all able to reflect on them.

I could. For a few years. The ones I spent in that house. I don't know if they were happy (the word "happy" is like a hole dug in dry sand), but it'd be fair to say those years shook us up. They were a tense kind of education without origin or destination. That's it. Those years were the shake-up.

I guess there are those who might—in retrospect—take it as a sign of what was to come and point to symptoms as if they'd known all along, who might toss out a few quips about how anger and rebellion were crushed under the weight of fanaticism and repetition. Fact. But I don't think in those terms. That's all fine for Smithfield and the rest of them, who believed there was something more behind all that wonder of shared experience, something that was always about to happen but never fully took shape, a wave that was going to wash everything away, even the Big Concert, the Big Trip, and the Big Party. Everything. Something was finally going to arrive or awaken, something that already hummed in the air around that mass of warm, tangled bodies, something written in capital letters. We already know how it ended. In total degradation. Disorientation, all those people glued to the screens of their computers or their cell phones; dudes who wander the streets filthy with their dogs and call themselves anarchists but who shake in their boots at just the thought of sharing something (an idea, a word) with their neighbors. It ended in those groups out in the woods. Young people who don't know how to be young. Some beacon of hope they are.

Back then, though, they'd show up at the house unannounced. They came from both coasts, from the south, from the border. Whenever an argument finally became the last, whenever the loaf of bread someone had been saving for breakfast turned out to be full of worms, whenever the usual needling stirred an angst that had been building up for years, anytime some kid got a little peek behind the curtain, the stage was set for them to hear about this mansion where scientists and artists experimented with their own bodies. Any old thing would light the fuse. And they'd take off without a plan or a thought of turning back. They'd leave in the middle of their first college class, from a party that was getting boring, after that kiss in the back of a car they'd been waiting so long for, or in the small hours of the night as their parents dreamt of domestic tragedies. They were losing their children and they knew it. They were losing them but even so they kept up the lie called father or mother (which is nothing compared to the bigger lie, that ridiculous conjunction, "father and mother"). And the kids would show up at Bridgend with their backpack or their guitar on their shoulder, their clothes in tatters and their eyes burning with a drive they still didn't understand.

Most of them were Gabi's age. None of them were over nineteen, and some were younger (there was one sixteen-year-old who Clarke and Gutierrez took in and hid from his parents until the police came to get him). No one really knew who came and went, though. No one was keeping track. The only thing that mattered was preserving the sense of multitude, the heat of bodies in movement, the electricity of dozens of minds plunged into the ocean that our own reasoning had expelled us from, dozens of individualities finally liberated from the weight of their names and synchronized into a single being thanks to LSD. I'd been there since the beginning, I'd watched the group swell from a few members and their brilliant guides to an organism that just kept growing, and it always surprised me how the kids who rang the fancy doorbell at the Clarke mansion grew younger and younger.

That should have been our warning. It was only logical they'd discover after just a few days that the Big Party wasn't going to cut it, that it wasn't enough to live on the fringes of society. They wanted to shake things up, or to burn it all down if necessary. "You never know what is enough unless you know what is more than enough." If that's so, then those kids were the wisest on earth.

Gabi had just turned eighteen when she arrived. She'd waited an eternity to be able to legally slam the door in her mother's face ("It's better to kill a baby in the cradle than to raise it with frustrated desires"). She told the guy who opened the door that she wanted to sing. But she didn't say it like that. "Hi, I'm Gabi Brown. Let the music play" were her exact words. You'd have to be born four or five decades ago to be able to say that to a stranger with total impunity. I dare you to try it today: you wouldn't get anything but a laugh, a shrug, or maybe some loose change.

She never did sing, though. Not in the Big Concert, at least. She sang for us, around bonfires in the winter, by the river in the summer, or accompanied by a guitar in the bedroom. And that's why she lingers on. In death, she's perfect. Smithfield and I, on the other hand, have been on the way out since then. Slowly, which has got to be the worst way to leave anywhere. Fact. Getting old is living between semicolons, without redeeming paragraph breaks. Getting old is giving up intensity.

I was twenty-seven or twenty-eight (or maybe a hundred and twenty, and I just didn't notice). That number didn't mean anything to me, because we all counted our age from our second birth, that is, from the first time we took LSD. Mine was in a cabin in the middle of the woods, with Clarke, Gutierrez, Frank, and two kids younger than me who'd never done it before, either. They gave it to us diluted in orange juice. Frank had already done it a few times, but later he said it was different that day. His perception of light and color wasn't as important. That day, he felt like he couldn't coordinate his movements, like his mind had suddenly found itself trapped in the body of a three-year-old. Clarke and Gutierrez limited themselves to taking notes. They also recorded part of the session, the part where they were able to keep us inside the cabin, at least. One of the younger guys climbed out the window, ran down the hill and onto a farm, stole some eggs and threw them in the air ("I wanted to see them fly," he explained later), and then collapsed under a tree, where he took off his clothes and chewed through part of his sweater (he said that the purple wool had seemed like a bottomless bowl of sugared raspberries). The other one lay down in the corner with a book and stayed like that. When Clarke and Gutierrez asked him to describe what he saw, he said that there was a man inside the letters who ran from line to line and made it hard for him to read. Don't ask me what book it was. Something about a doomed family.

I didn't feel any of that. For me, everything was simple and incredibly clear: I understood the inner workings of the world. I can still do it, if I focus on remembering that ray of intensity. The way that kid ran, for example, seemed like a masterpiece of engineering. I could have explained which muscles he was using, which tendons and ligaments, if I'd only known what

they were called. Then there was how Frank, who was lying on
the floor on the far side of the room, was playing with a coin.
It seemed like he thought he'd discovered a secret. I thought
so, too: the secret that connects form and material. So powerful and so simple, the nickel could have been alive. And you
know what, it was. Or, at least, it was as long as I was looking
at it. Same thing happened to Huxley with some flowers in a
vase. An iris and a rose, I think. A living being captured at the
moment of its greatest power, which is also the moment of its
decline. The glory of finitude. That's what I call the shake-up.
Fact: drugs will open anyone's eyes; the question is where we
choose to look.

Not albaria. Albaria closes your eyes and sets you down in
a ray of light where time doesn't exist. An animal time where
consciousness disappears. Imagine living entirely inside yourself. Imagine reading the trace of your prey on a poplar leaf
and clamping down on it like a piece of meat; imagine being
the scent and the receptors that translate it into an instinct.
Imagine recovering the ability to predict rain, to hunt an animal by its tracks, to hunt and fail, to hunt and despair, to hunt
and ride the urgency of a nameless drive, to be one with it all
and then touch the skin of a lover with new fingers, a skin
made of textures and flavors your body reacts to without
words to trip it up, divinely turned inward, with no awareness
of mortality or your own gradual withering to tarnish that
time—that moment when something like innocence, or sav-
agery, is finally recovered.

It was evil. But it was ours. That knowledge, that life in
present tense. It was ours and we were cast out of it. All the
religions know it. They know it and they hide it from us. How
could that effect not drive you insane? Once Gabi figured out
how to make the seeds Gutierrez had brought back from the

islands multiply, she began experimenting with albaria non-stop. She did some pretty strange things, and she hadn't learned them all with us. When she arrived at Bridgend, she already smoked marijuana every day. That wasn't a problem. But she'd also tried other things, and she knocked back whiskey like an Irish cop in a bad movie. She said she'd started drinking in middle school, when her mother realized how beautiful she'd gotten. She never forgave Gabi for that beauty. I can't say I blame her: when Cecilia Brown showed up at Bridgend to take the girl who Gabi and the rest of us called Celeste, but who she probably rebaptized with some awful name, no one could believe Gabi had come out of those colossal hips, those greasy curls plastered to skin, that Queen-of-Swords demeanor.

No. Gabi was different, a foreigner among her own family. But also among us. Most people in the group just wanted to follow their urges, escape their own minds. Children do this naturally all the time: they spin until they're dizzy. Saints, too (make themselves dizzy, I mean). There's no need to resort to substances. Extreme pain or pleasure can be entrancing or illuminating, too. That's what it was about for most of them. See how far they could go. Truth is, martyrs walk side by side into the arena, but they're crucified alone. That's what Frank called Gabi. A martyr of psychedelia.

I, on the other hand, think Gabi's brain was fried before she even left home. There's really no overstating the effect that the biggest lie can have on an impressionable girl. Instead of finding refuge in games, books, or television, she'd turned to pamphlets and pseudoscientific magazines. She'd read all about Eastern philosophy and religions, esoterica, and UFOs, but her eighteen-year-old brain could only absorb information in the most structureless, confused way. She could be an unbelievable bore. She'd preach. At Bridgend she developed her own "meditation practice," based on a kind of Buddhism where you reflect on things in different stages of decomposition. Before you knew it, she had a group of acolytes she'd take on walks to observe how something was always dying out there. That was around when she adopted a lapdog and a deer Clarke had found next to its dead mother on the side of the highway. The animals ate what she ate, and once we even found her sleeping with them in their pen. I guess it was part of her "philosophy," which also included infrequent bathing and sharing dishes and ticks with her pets.

Everything was different before Gabi arrived. Those were harmonious years but, like I said, they also shook us up. Frank and I moved to Bridgend right after my rebirth. Gutierrez had "recruited" us both at college: he needed kids for an experiment with substances. He wanted to classify the hallucinations they produced. I'd never been a very serious student. I took psychology, physics, Third World art, the most popular classes or the ones no one wanted, I didn't care. Maybe because it had taken me so much to get there (I had two jobs to pay for my classes and I got a certain pleasure out of squandering my money and my health on knowledge, on always being just on the verge of defining myself, of finding myself, but not quite). Until Gutierrez showed up with his rich friends who'd decided to finance the Great Liberation. Frank and I traded our classes for an education at Bridgend. We believed that diplomas and certificates were part of the problem, not the solution. That it was time for the true spirit, which wasn't going to reveal itself in any lecture hall. Time to drink turpentine in cheap hotels, time for alcohol and dick and endless dancing.

For me, those were years of grace, of real thinking (I don't think now; now I'm too worried about chewing). Those years were like an offering Someone dropped in my lap out of guilt for all the empty hours that would follow. Empty the way only time spent far from truth can be, a time that's not even decline or decrepitude but an alien, parallel state where the soul spins, brutally alone. Asteroid 7998, alias Berilia X. Off course since 1969.

Smithfield knows it, even now in his hospital bed. It's how he saw me every day in the museum: wayward. He could see me as I really was, dead and empty, the same way I saw him. That's why he insisted on talking about the past. On making amends. That's why he convinced me to form this group that seems nothing like our community back then, that extraordinary organism we built and destroyed without even realizing it.

ↀ

"The reason we can't adopt you is simple."

Omar put his right arm around Halley's shoulder. They both leaned over the counter and looked at her seriously. Berenice took another sip of the tea with milk and spices that she'd ordered after carefully studying the menu. They'd served it to her in a big white mug with a thick rim where her lips enjoyed lingering, a mug where it seemed life might have begun once, as if it had once been full of the amoeba soup they talked about in magazines.

Omar kept talking.

"The thing is, it's not just me and Halley. Before we met, she had a terrible case of wanderlust and I had dozens of phobias. We're still the same. Love doesn't cure any of that. But it does create a third presence that surrounds it all. We call it the Entity. It's fragile, jealous. It won't allow any kind of guest. We have to take very good care of it. That's why we decided not to have children. It's the same with the dropouts. We sympathize (we've had more than one conversation with them over a slice of pumpkin pie), but we know the woods aren't for us."

Halley nodded, lowered her eyes to reveal the gray eye shadow on their lids, and adjusted the stud glinting above her right eyebrow.

"Omar probably told you already that we believe in unrestricted circulation. People pass freely through this place, and that's what keeps it alive. It's a stop along the way, that's all. People should be like that, too. Stops along the way, I mean." She paused, stared intently at something in the air in front of her, and then, turning to Omar, said, "But we're telling it wrong, without any of the romance," and leaned toward him until her forehead touched her boyfriend's curls.

Berenice had never seen them like that. They were always washing containers, stirring pots, or talking with customers in that dreamlike state they walked around in, which she suddenly understood was probably an effect of the Entity they'd been talking about. Just like the boy in the bubble in that old movie, Omar and Halley saw the world through a transparent barrier that protected them but also kept everyone else at a distance.

Plastic people. Only half on their rockers. They would have been perfect, thought Berenice. She returned the empty mug to its saucer, slid off the stool, said goodbye to the couple, and, pretending to be more composed than she was, stepped back into the cold of the street.

Now it really was time to go see the Sphinxes. There was something calming about those stone beings. When things got bad, she'd head for Harry Winter's mausoleum and sit between the bare-breasted Egyptian-style statues. From there she could climb the hill diagonally to visit Liliana Amato's crypt, hidden among the pines, which looked like a dollhouse and had the nicest epitaph in the whole cemetery. Back down the hill, at a point that formed a triangle with the other two, was the tomb with no name: a miniature Gothic church, black and conquered by the advancing ivy, with an angel standing watch on the roof, sword held high.

Berenice didn't talk to the dead; she left that for Emma Lynn, who went to the Family's obelisk at least once a month to sit and chat for hours with Great-grandma Cecilia. It was the only tomb around that always had flowers on it.

Back then, the apartment was full of flowerpots and glass vases. Emma Lynn would set pansies, centaury, or freesias on the kitchen table, on the mantel above the decorative fireplace, and even on the floor next to the sofa or in the bathroom, between bottles of perfume and piles of cosmetics. From their vases, the flowers would draw the dark air from the furniture and send it back out so blue it was like living in another country or swimming in outer space. Berenice missed those days, when she'd come home from school and step into the suffocating love of those flowers. She missed those days when Emma Lynn was pretty and her only cares were the weddings, anniversaries, and holidays that always flooded the shop with orders.

Back then, they'd bring bouquets of forget-me-nots when they visited Great-grandma Cecilia. There were two stories about the flower and Berenice always managed to get her mother to tell both each time they went. God showed up in the first one, so they ran through it quickly as soon as they stepped through the front gate: when God made the earth, He gave a name to every living thing except for a bunch of little blue flowers that, when they realized they'd been unfairly left without a name, they called out in a tiny voice (that was nonetheless perfectly audible for the Almighty), "Forget me not!

Forget me not!" (no one knows why the flowers yelled twice). Surprised, God reviewed his list of names and realized that every single one had already been assigned, so he called the flower what it had shouted.

The second story was longer. It took place in France, or Poland, or Uruguay, or in any of those countries where people had manners, and it was about a courtship. One day, a gentleman put on a suit of armor to impress a young lady and invited her on a walk through the woods. When they arrived at the bank of a river, he discovered a cluster of blue flowers. As anyone in his situation would, he decided to pick a bouquet for the woman walking beside him (who perhaps should have been more focused on the drama about to unfold before her eyes). The gentleman leaned over the flowers, but his armor was so heavy that he fell into the river and drowned. Before he died, he tossed the bouquet to his beloved and shouted, above the roar of the water, "Forget me not! Forget me not!" No one knows why, but he shouted twice, too. Emma Lynn would cup her hands around her mouth and make her voice rise and fall in ridiculous scales before fading into an exaggerated cough, which kept them laughing at least as long as it took them to pass General Winnebiddle's tomb, with its miniature cannon and its list of battles.

Despite the two inane biographies they've carried since time immemorial, forget-me-nots were happy for a long time, especially during the wars, when they caught on among women waiting for their lovers to return from the front. When there were no more wars, or rather, when there were no more women waiting for someone to return, the flower grew popular among the dead and even rivaled lilies of the valley as a sign that man's memory worked better than the Creator's.

Emma Lynn used to say that if you forgot about your dead,

you turned them into corpses. People didn't know how much responsibility they held. The dead were bare, powerful names stripped of anecdotes and arguments, forever wrapped up in the lives of the living. Corpses needed no further explanation: they were the stuff of worms and those black bugs with long, glossy bodies that stretch their antennas over the stones and monuments that people think will improve the final resting place of their kin.

Cecilia Brown's grave didn't have any of those things. It was a simple headstone marked with her name and the date of her death (no one, not even she, knew when she was born), in stark contrast with the rest of the Family's circle: even the babies lay crushed under stone coffins that imitated the real ones below (certainly made of marble, mahogany, and bronze), where their skeletons slept for all eternity. Some had a Grecian urn at the head of their tomb. Thomas Klink, buried at the center, right next to the obelisk, had a statue of a woman holding a book open before a girl whose bows and skirt were being whipped around by the wind.

For Berenice, the Klink family slept in those stone beds. Especially the children. There were eight of them. She liked imagining their faces and the games they played back in nineteen-hundred-who-knows-what—the names and dates had faded from their headstones. That hadn't happened with the adults. Emma Lynn explained to her that at some point the Family had renovated the tombs (assuming that something like a tomb could, in fact, be renovated). They had replaced the cement headstones on the adults' graves with polished granite. Nobody had thought it necessary to replace the ones that marked the graves of the eight children gone too soon.

Those children were the reason Cecilia Brown was buried in that cemetery for rich people, alongside a family with a different last name. Berenice's mother had told her that Cecilia had cared for all the young Klinks, and had even saved the life of one named Alvin, the heir. The rest had been taken by the same congenital disorder. Cecilia Brown knew as much about remedies and illnesses as she did about taming mischievous children. Next, Emma Lynn would shake her head (two magnificent curls hung over her eyes) and do something Berenice hated: she'd sit next to Cecilia's tomb and start listing all the problems Berenice was causing with her precocious intelligence. Her grandmother would listen in silence, but Emma Lynn always returned home wiser and armed with instructions for how to improve their daily life.

The flowers were part of those instructions. When Emma Lynn lost her job at Mr. Müller's pharmacy, it was everything Cecilia had taught her about flowers that came to her rescue. The wave of economic depression—as journalists who specialized in euphemisms described it—had actually begun almost twenty years earlier. Except it wasn't a wave so much as an ocean, and the whole region was drowning. Convinced that hard work always wins out, people refused to admit that the city was turning into a film set; its cathedrals went up for sale and its factories shut down, and both attracted vandals and the dispossessed the way large animals draw parasites to themselves. The steelworks was the first to close. Then came the offices of the oil and gas company that had been housed in the city's tallest building, and then the tomato sauce plant, the conservatory, and the two biggest theaters. Only the university and the museum survived. And the farms and the organic grocers: in the midst of the crisis, people clung even more tightly to healthy living than in other parts of the country. They stopped vaccinating their children and buying aspirin, antibiotics, or vitamins, but they never stopped marking the important days of their lives with bouquets. That was how, when the pharmacy closed its doors forever, Emma convinced Mr. Müller to let her try a flower shop.

Berenice had never seen her mother as energetic as she'd been those last two years. The farmers started coming by twice a week to sell their blue hydrangeas, angel trumpets, and white lupins. With these common, practically wild flowers, Emma would make municipal bouquets in the city's colors. She had regular customers, including several officials who never forgot the requisite wreaths and decorations. She also ordered seeds and bulbs by mail. They arrived from all across the country and beyond. Part of the shop was full of flowerpots where grafted plants flourished alongside other experiments based on things Emma learned in books and from the secrets her dead grandmother shared with her. After months of trial and error, she achieved a blue carnation that made her famous in the world of flower arrangements and sold for a lot of money at a public auction. In the end, the old man from the museum got it. He'd won a bidding war against a woman from the cooking club, who walked away grumbling with a run-of-the-mill bergenia.

Before the auction, Emma had already expanded Mr. Müller's garage and added a nursery. Berenice wished her mother had never gotten tired of flowers, that she'd stuck with making decorations, that the secret of their effects had remained locked away forever in their cycles of beauty and decay.

When she reached that point in her memories, Berenice interrupted her walk to the cemetery to look in the window of a shop that sold security cameras. It was one of the few stores left on the street. Long ago, Grandville Avenue had been one of the city's main thoroughfares. There had been a beauty parlor that specialized in manicures where some nice women from Thailand worked, and a shop that sold knickknacks. But they'd moved downtown. Only a business like Emma's could survive in that wasteland. The only signs of life on Grandville Avenue were the camera and computer store and, a little farther down, a bar called the Graveyard, where a few bikers and pool sharks went.

There was nothing to see in the window display, but it was getting dark and Berenice needed to think. It had been nearly five days since her mother disappeared, but that was less important than what she had done last summer. That's when the real transformation happened, the transition from flowers to teas, concoctions, and salves. If she could uncover the secret behind that change, her mother's departure would surely present itself as its obvious, necessary outcome. But the key to that mystery wasn't in apartment seven on Edmond Street. It must be in the flower shop.

Berenice had passed by on the afternoon of the first day, but she hadn't searched the place thoroughly. She'd only stuck her head inside, a bit daunted by how indifferent the plants seemed to her mother's absence. Maybe Emma Lynn was still there, or was on her way back. But the spark this possibility had ignited in her heart almost died when she thought about it more carefully. The plants would be in terrible shape after going so long without water. What if her mother was testing her, and her disappearance was simply a way of seeing whether she, Berenice, could be left in charge of her paradise? What if when she opened the door she found Emma Lynn hidden behind the folding screen, ready to leap out with an accusatory finger pointed at her? The idea sent a shiver up her spine. Her mother believed in flowers the same way Berenice believed in water. Her idea of the Great Beyond was a wild, unexplored garden that she could walk around for all eternity and still never figure out its design. That was her idea of happiness. And Berenice knew it, even though they'd never talked about it. She knew it and she'd forgotten. Instead of making her sad, this discovery brought a smile to her face. She stopped and retraced her steps, heading away from the corner where she should have turned toward home. When she got to the next intersection, she quickened her pace until she was running down the street: the possibility that she'd failed one of Emma Lynn's stupid tests was infinitely better than the task of becoming a left-behind.

5

It wasn't a song. It was a dry, unsettling murmur, far removed from the complexity of language, a single phrase she repeated (he was sure of it) by humming deep in her chest, eyes closed and fingers laced across her belly.

Vik sat back down on the carpet, facing the closet door.

He couldn't call the police. He wasn't one of those people who could dial three little numbers and, at the speed of television, find themselves in the right. Anything would be better than having to deal with the authorities, who would read his accent, his skin, and his home like signs and see him (not the woman) as the prime suspect. Besides, the police were famous for their brutality. He'd seen them at it too many times: harassing pedestrians, demanding identification in bars, and doing who-knew-what in those big trucks of theirs. He imagined they would do more than just kick her out. They probably had special places set up for people like her. Institutions. Like the farms where they put the left-behinds to work.

He considered, for a moment, calling the technician who had installed the security cameras. He would know what to do. He was a tall man, pink skinned and clean-shaven, and just pudgy enough to not seem too militaristic. He inspired confidence. The confidence of infomercials. Of a Bob or a Tom. Of "Do It Yourself" and of every man who ever held a weapon (no matter whether it was a revolver, a drill, or a set of pruning shears). But calling the technician would have meant accepting his defeat, his complete ignorance of the rules of the game, and the strange and unsettling activity of his hormones.

Inside, she was singing.

The women of Coloma used to sing, too. Not anymore. Not even in his memory. Now half the island was covered in ash, lava, and volcanic rock. You could still go there, if you found a guide who knew the old city and was daring enough to show you around "the Pompeii of the Caribbean." That was what the websites were calling it, in an attempt to dignify the catastrophe with new revenue streams. Vik believed in them. He believed in tourism, in *souvenirs*, in anything that defied the no-fly zone declared by a government that had temporarily relocated to the north of the island. He believed there was still hope as long as people visited the ruins. He wasn't sure what was left to hope for, but sometimes, when his back pain kept him awake at night, he would stare at those websites (run by illegal travel agencies hawking extreme tourism, or bloggers who collected "the world's best ghost towns") with images of people strolling across that sea of dry, gray earth where the town hall's rooftop used to be, snapping photos beside the clock on its dome, or sitting next to the cathedral bell. Once, he stumbled across some pictures taken from a boat. You could see the part of the pier where the women had sung (songs without origin or end, songs so innocent they were as much lullabies as elegies). Another time, he'd seen a piano covered with ash. If he strained to peer through the window behind the instrument, he could see one of the mansions set into the side of the mountain. There had been a forest there, once, and in it was the path that led up to his parents' summer home.

Each discovery was assigned a place on Vik's hard drive as he went about reconstructing a map of that city buried in rock and ash. With total impunity, as if he were just anyone, Vik would visit "one of the most chilling websites in the world," where he would click on dozens of images in which, even in two dimensions and in the anonymous glow of the screen, a trace of him still existed.

Yes. The women of Coloma used to sing. But not like her: her song wasn't innocent. It was premeditated. Malicious. As if she were naked. He suddenly realized he wasn't to blame for imagining her like that. She was the one who telegraphed it, through the ferocity with which she chose to take shelter. To which she chose to reduce herself. The only thing between them, aside from the door, was that melody—like a warning, a mockery, or a last resort.

Vik tried to concentrate on the practical side of the issue. He stared at the doorknob. He'd never really looked at it before. It was round, made of metal, and had a little lock at its center. That made no sense. Why would someone install a door with a lock like that in a closet? He turned it again, gently this time, just enough to feel the resistance. Inside, the song wavered momentarily. Yes, the knob clearly had a lock, with a little button that could be turned from inside. So it was just a matter of finding the key.

He remembered the blue metal box that the former owner had left on a shelf in the basement. The man had repeated several times that the house Vik was buying was one hundred percent safe. For years, he had rented it out to students, strangers living with strangers who had devised cohabitation strategies that would have made a prison warden proud: they limited their activities to their forty-square-foot bedrooms, inhaled their food to reduce verbal exchanges to a bare minimum, and stuck labels on everything, even fruit preserves. It was no surprise they eventually demanded locks on all the doors, but Vik hadn't imagined that could include the closets. The man (clearly another Bob or Tom) had probably bought the door-knobs on sale and installed them at the same time. The key to that door might be in the blue box with all the others (the one to the tool shed in the garden that Vik never set foot in; the one to the garage, which had been converted into storage for his completed projects; the one to the medicine cabinet).

Thinking of the basement, Vik also remembered the Ploucquet he'd brought home from the museum a few days earlier: *Romeo and Juliet by Moonlight*. It was still on his worktable, wait-ing for him. Transporting it hadn't been easy. He hadn't been able to find a box big enough, so he'd needed to wrap it in paper, set it on the back seat of a taxi, and convince the driver to go as slowly as possible (the string holding the candelabra in the Capulets' ballroom was frayed). The entire piece was pretty damaged. Being shipped so many times had destroyed Romeo's outstretched arm and the treetops around that noble house of Verona. Juliet, a rat of pinkish hue (Romeo was a white mouse), seemed to be in pretty good shape, though her tulle dress and brass crown would need to be replaced. Her father, on the other hand, who was carefully hidden behind another of the second-floor windows, had lost his hat, and a few mildew stains darkened his face.

It had been hard to defend the Ploucquets after Smith-field fell ill. The repository couldn't hold any more, and every month he discovered that the museum's directors had chosen a new piece to send to the incinerator. The heyday of taxi-dermy was coming to an end. Now, all people wanted from a museum of natural history was entertainment, light shows, robots, and mechanical dinosaurs. It made perfect sense that the Ploucquets—with their combination of innocence and obscenity so typical of the Victorians—would be the first target of this cleansing. Vik had begun taking them home without thinking through what he would do when he ran out of space. Aside from the one he had in the drawing room (*Rabbit with Watch*), there were four in the garage and two in the basement. He calculated that he had room for ten more, give or take, depending on their size.

It was hard to explain why he couldn't let them be destroyed. It was different with other pieces (several birds had suffered that fate, as did the Nevada jackalope, widely considered one of Ferrán Spring's greatest achievements). This wasn't professional dedication, either. His feelings for the Ploucquets were something else.

One of the world's greatest taxidermists, William Hornaday, used to say that the sight of an animal—living or dead—always moved him deeply. From that first shudder in the presence of a form so different from your own, it was a short step to admiration and from there to affection. The same was not true of humans: it took real effort to love one of your own kind. There was so little to admire there, aside from greater symmetry, an idiosyncrasy or a defect that made up for your own. Smithfield half jokingly called this feeling the passion of the taxidermist: the deep emotion that became a driving need to exert control over that other form, over its balance points and secret articulations, over the structures and mechanisms that accounted for that other harmony. That was the only way you could throw yourself into the work of removing organs, draining arteries, and stretching hides over wooden skeletons. But something was lost on the way to that understanding. No matter how well the preservation was executed, in the end something was always missing. Not from the animal's body, which could simulate with absolute precision the leap of a predator or the horror of the prey, but rather from that of its new owner, who relinquished part of their own internal harmony as payment for having taken a rare trophy from the cycle of decomposition that was life.

Vik had never experienced the passion of the taxidermist. Not in Hornaday's terms. But the Ploucquets were different. He saw himself reflected in those miniatures, in the attempt not just to simulate life but to go beyond it, to transform it into something else. He had been looking forward to restoring Romeo and his trees all week. And there he was, sitting in front of his closet, caught in an impossible situation, losing the few working hours his body allowed him.

He got to his feet carefully but couldn't keep the wooden floor under the carpet from creaking. Inside, the woman moved toward the door. The song did not stop. In fact, it got louder and faster, as if accompanying the tension in the body from which it surged. Vik thought he could hear the air enter her nose in the pause just before she would begin the phrase again. He imagined her with her ear pressed to the wood, hanging off each of his movements. Maybe she could even see him through some crack he hadn't noticed.

∝

Because you couldn't call this a group. It's just a random assortment of individuals. The first one to show up was Elizabeth, Ron Duda's wife. She wanted revenge, of course. She was wearing jeans, leather boots, and a baseball cap. The boots must have been her husband's. Tough to walk through the woods in shoes four sizes too big, I thought. Apparently,

I was going to have to start with the basics. But I didn't say anything. I tried to put on my best face (my best face remembers that twill dress; my best face, if it tries hard enough, can even imitate the one Frank looked at with a little affection back then). We met here. Well, not in this exact room. In the wood-paneled living room of the Community Center for Senior Citizens. Our "club." Our "haven." More like our waiting room, because we don't do anything there but kill time. A place to do yoga, play cards, throw "socials," or do any other activity that distracts us from our natural state of waiting to die. And to think, some societies actually chose to be gerontocracies. Fact. If someone were to come to this group of elders for advice, these old folks who spend their days shuffling through dance lessons, drooling in front of the television, and airing their oldest grievances (how many stories about fishing, talented grandchildren, holes in one . . . how many arguments about denture glue can a woman take?), they'd walk out with a sure-fire plan for mass stupidification.

But no one would think of doing anything like that. It's all about "keeping busy," and "having a good time." Piling on tactics of diversion. They said they hired a Dominican lady to teach the cha-cha this year. I had expected some young thing, but no: she's a voluminous sixty-year-old black woman. Adela or Estela. She must be pretty fat, because she brought her own chair (double-wide, red plush), from which, they say, she leads class by banging a wooden staff against the floor to keep time.

A Hungarian psychiatrist visits us, too, once a week. "To chat." She's very popular. Especially with the men. I mention it in case you all don't know, but I'm pretty sure you do. She can't be over fifty. She's tall and thin and has big blue eyes. Her name is Isabel Danko and she talks with a thick accent. Actually, these videos were her idea; she was the one who brought in the technicians and set up the "memory room" or "time capsule." Of course, she had to go and ruin it with a bunch of explanations about the therapeutic effects of words, about society's need to preserve our stories for future generations, and about people's interest in them. Did you catch that, Doc? By the way, you should do something about that accent— they have classes for that, you know. And don't worry about giving us "social" rationales. You don't have to convince us at all: just provide a camera, a private room, and a few technical pointers, and you'll have no shortage of old folks willing—no, desperate—to record their life stories. Not for posterity, not for their children's children. Not even for themselves. They'll do it just to hear the sound of their own voice, to prove that air is still passing through that heap of bones, that their organs still serve their most basic functions. But none of this is news to you. It's the same story, over and over. The mirror stage turns back on itself. Fact. We're like little kids: give us some attention, and we'll dance for anyone.

That explains why they always line up at her table. You know, Dr. Danko never comes to the center without her gilded black porcelain tea set. The first thing she does when she arrives is take the cups and saucers out of her bag; she does it ceremoniously, slowly, like a child getting ready for a tea party with her dolls. Then, she goes to the kitchen and comes back with the essential component: the teapot, which has a castle painted on it and steams with whatever concoction she's offering her interlocutors. A nice organic tea, Hungarian, it seems. She's also pretty liberal with the prescriptions. She puts on a good act, and I think almost everyone has sat down with her at one point or another. It's like none of them was ever part of a revolution. Not me. I know what's up: it's all about keeping us docile. About turning us into the Learned Council of Gerontozombies. That's why I agreed to sit in front of this camera every Monday. I already had my dose of docility, thank you very much, back in the Bridgend days. I knew long before what happened with Gabi that, given where we are in our evolution, vigilance is the only option. We have to stay sharp. Now more than ever. If you're depressed, go outside and scream. Knock something over, run someone over. Better that than the pills. Better that than the lie.

The first thing I did that Saturday was grill Elizabeth about the buck in question. She said she hadn't been able to get a good look at him. The only thing she could say for sure was that the animal was huge and that it shook its head from side to side as it ran, like it'd gone crazy. She'd never seen another deer run like that (living so close to the woods, she'd had plenty of chances to observe them). It reminded her of a horse trying to shake its bridle. It seemed, she said, like the buck was trying to get something off its head. A powerful image. Seemed important. Aside from that, Elizabeth could only remember the metallic smell of blood, the shattered cereal bowls, and her fingers dialing 911.

Tears were inevitable. I asked her about the scar. She said she hadn't been close enough to the animal to see it clearly, but that it looked like the mark a rope would leave, as if it had been in captivity for a while. I wrote it all down. It made sense for us to have a concrete goal. That way, once they had trained enough, I could take them into the woods for more than just practice. I was going to teach them to track, stalk, and land a deer, and Ron Duda's buck would be the perfect target.

Five more people showed up that day. I'd scheduled the meeting for noon to keep out the bingo players and the unimaginative retirees who would've gotten themselves involved in some organized activity by that point. That way

I'd be sure to get only the ones who were genuinely interested. I wanted a motivated group formed by natural selection: none of those compulsive gamblers or seniors who get up at four to wait—fully dressed, breakfast eaten—for the shops to open, for the free guitar lesson to begin, or for someone to show up from the animal shelter looking for volunteers. (A real sweet deal: now that you've spent the best years of your life working, why not relax by doing some free labor for the city?)

The Armstrong sisters were next. They were wearing the same housedresses and wool jackets as always, ankle-strap shoes with low heels, and a thick layer of makeup on their faces. I was surprised that they wanted to learn to hunt, though they did spend more time in the center than almost anyone, usually fighting over the flower arrangements or waiting their turn at Dr. Danko's table. When I grilled them about their motives, they said they'd always hated deer. Margaret told me that when she was young a white-tailed doe would watch her through her bedroom window every night. There was nothing gentle or maternal about its gaze. Just the opposite: the doe was stalking her. Maggie was convinced that the animal wanted to take her to the underworld, just like they'd done with several miners from the area (according to local folklore, down there the deer reign, trapping and torturing any miner who ventures too far). Maggie grew up a nervous, irritable insomniac with a single goal in life: to live as far as possible from the woods. A lot of good it did her. A year ago, right after Heather got surgery to fix her varicose veins, a frenzied buck came crashing through the window of the intensive care unit. There were no serious injuries, but the sisters walked away surer than ever of the conspiracy. I welcomed them on board: I respect people who identify their personal crusade early on, however they do it. (We all have one, and only one, and the sooner we figure out what it is, the better.) Purpose and method, Berilia. That's what I always say. Otherwise, you're going nowhere fast.

Then came Tom and Betty Paz, the oldest in the group. He's eighty-two (I know because he went to school with my cousin, who'd be eighty-two if he were still alive). She's got to be at least ten years older, because I remember the scandal when they started dating. They had four sons, who are now scattered across the country. As long as his place in the world was determined by hours invested in money, you could say that Tom was an entrepreneur. But retirement made him a new man: he traveled all over, raced vintage cars, went scuba diving off the coast of Australia, and became the producer and star of a traveling theater company that staged Shakespeare plays in small towns. As long as her place in the world was determined by hours invested in money, you could say that Betty was beautiful. A real looker. Until the two of them blew their savings on their outrageous projects. Now they live off what their sons send them, in an enormous house they can barely maintain (I hear they have at least four bedrooms they never set foot in). It would probably be fair to say they're what kids today call a couple of fucking fossils, but they're the only ones with any experience: a few years ago, they went on safari in Africa and loved it.

Massimo Cercone was the fifth. He's short, at least thirty pounds overweight, and he smiles too much. There can't be many people worse suited to becoming a hunter. He used to be the best barber around. He had clients who lived in the suburbs but didn't shave or cut their hair in their own neighborhoods. They preferred to drive to Max's. The business is still running smoothly; his youngest son is in charge now. It's Max who's not running smoothly. As the years went by, the shaking in his hands got worse and worse until one day he was diagnosed with Parkinson's. When I asked him about his interest in hunting, he told me that he thought target practice might help with his condition. It seemed better not to say anything at the time, but I decided to keep a close eye on him. A man with uncontrollable tremors isn't exactly someone you want in your Rifles for Beginners class.

When it was time, I had them sit in a circle. Just like before. It was a different group of people and none of us could sit on the floor if we wanted to, but there was something in the air, a feeling of anticipation, like in the Bridgend days. Days that filled some of us with pride, and some with shame. To look at me now, you wouldn't imagine any of it: not the music, not the sex until dawn, and definitely not the minds freed in an attic decorated specifically for that purpose.

Maybe all Smithfield wanted was to relive those times. But he didn't say a word about any of that when he came. He didn't mention the day the world stood still. He stood at the center of the circle (in the same blue blazer he wore that day at the zoo), cleared his throat, and started talking about the deer.

꩜

Without breaking stride, Berenice ran to where the woods met the cemetery at the end of the street. From there, she'd have to climb a hill along a dirt path that would leave her right behind the nursery. That had been another of Emma's brilliant ideas. Her business sense surprised everyone, even Mr. Müller. Because of its location, her shop was able to capitalize both on mourners visiting their dead and on people coming out of the woods, whether they were farmers selling flowers and bulbs, or the suburban neo-hippies who bought infusions of all kinds, poultices for their wrinkles, herbs, and seeds to sprinkle on their cereal. No one saw more clearly than Emma the potential clients in those "natural" women who seemed totally unfazed by the passing of time, but who would rush out to buy Emma-lina the minute they turned thirty. In fact, it was her mother's first wrinkles that inspired the mix of cucumber and herbs the two of them later baptized with that name.

Unlike the apartment on Edmond Street, the nursery and flower shop were always clean and tidy. Emma Lynn hadn't worried too much about fixing up Mr. Müller's garage, except for building a rectangular room onto the back. She kept the cement floors and cut windows out of the side walls, where she hung two stained-glass panels she'd bought from a church that was being demolished. She hadn't planned the design. One day she just stopped into the church and bought them on a whim (business was already booming, even though the shop was just a table set up in a garage). She'd needed to figure out the size and shape of the windows to accommodate the huge, colorful round panels and their patterns of stars or flowers repeating in an infinite symmetry. The effect was like being in an iridescent underwater capsule where Berenice could have lived, if it weren't for all those plants.

Some days, the silence of the plants was too much for her to bear. It wasn't like a human's: it was the silence of growth, reproduction, and death condensed into infinitesimal time and space. Sometimes, just to disrupt her awareness of all the effort going on around her, Berenice would let out a shriek from her chair. Her mother would look up with raised eyebrows from the bouquet she was working on and say only, "Again?"

"Uh-huh," Berenice would answer, and go back to her note-book.

The two of them spent endless hours in the flower shop, Berenice sitting at the table in the nursery and Emma Lynn wrapped up in her project of the moment. The famous blue carnation crowned her achievements, but Berenice vividly remembered the failures that had preceded it: a thornless Marie van Houtte that ended up as an undersized bush with sickly flowers; a tricolor cactus that died in its early stages of development; and a cross between Sri Lankan and Mexican varieties of plumeria that produced a flowerless, sticky-leafed tree, which was still growing out behind the nursery. Berenice knew that, in that world, achievement came only after months and months of experiments, and that a single specimen, freed from the laws of nature, was like a shooting star: impossible to re-create. There was no guarantee that another could be produced just like it, or that the same method would work on a different plant. All this fascinated her, but she lacked Emma Lynn's passion for detail, her ability to recognize the traits common to species so different in size and color that they seemed to come from different planets. Even Purple Queen was a challenge. Despite everything her mother had taught her about bonsai, the tree was always on the verge either of death or of rampant growth (Berenice forgot that pruning, rather than watering, was key). They'd had several arguments about it, in which Berenice insisted that overwatering was part of her system and not the result of impatience. Emma Lynn eventually left her alone. She'd never cared much for bonsai, and seemed glad Berenice had picked an area she found uninspiring and sometimes even repulsive.

The problem with miniature trees wasn't just that they required absolute dedication. Chance would intervene at the most unlikely moment and, no matter how careful you had been, the result might be something inelegant, monstrous. Even some of the best bonsai, the ones featured in books and on websites, seemed to Emma Lynn like small creatures being tortured. This was no surprise, coming from someone who loved ivy, ferns, and towering conifers. Berenice, on the other hand, liked to push her creations to the limit. Just like her dolls, Purple Queen was going to be one of a kind. The idea fascinated her.

What she liked most about flowers, though, was naming them. For that reason alone, she encouraged her mother to create one that could be called *Jazzy Turquoise, Berenicis igniae,* or *Bluebell berenicii.* Finding the right name, one that really captured the flower's essence, felt like a matter of principle; if there was one thing that made Berenice angry, it was the sheer number of plants that were named after botanists or, worse, French soldiers. What on earth did Magnol's double chin and curly wig have to do with a creature that had been around longer than bees, and which, in a marvel of adaptation, developed fleshy leaves so it could be pollinated by beetles? She was completely indifferent to her mother's explanations of how important the botanist had been. Emma Lynn insisted that Magnol deserved recognition because he had taken it upon himself to prove that plants also had lineages, which meant that not everything in Genesis could be taken literally. Also, she went on, it wasn't as if Magnol committed the sin of botanical self-aggrandizement. It was his disciples who had baptized the magnolia, despite the fact that American tribes already had several beautiful names for it. How much better, thought Berenice, did *talauma* or *yoloxochitl* sound. With those names, the flower forgot all about explorers and encyclopedias, and went back to being the tree of myth that it deserved to be. She could spend hours listening to the botanical tales Emma Lynn had memorized or read out loud from *The Big Book of Flowers,* which she kept on the bottom shelf behind the counter.

Her mother wasn't particularly interested in names. She didn't give them to the plants, and the shop didn't have business cards or an awning, just a sign out front with the words "Flowers, Plants and More, Ask for Emma Lynn" written in peeling paint. She had only agreed to call the blue carnation *Gloria artificialis* because Berenice had insisted that it would help at the auction. Emma Lynn had decided that month to try cultivating orchids. The carnation was a small price to pay for the challenge of mastering those difficult flowers.

The auction had been Mr. Müller's idea, and he helped post flyers and announcements in the few places people still gathered in the city—teahouses where women exchanged recipes and boredom; art galleries, cafés, and a few churches. The event was a success. Even Omar and Halley were there, with a few of their artist friends. Emma Lynn decorated the whole shop in blue. Berenice helped out by serving gingersnaps tinted the same color. They placed the *Gloria artificialis* on a stool in a dark corner, under a glass dome that split the lamplight into dozens of rays. Many people were interested, but no one offered as much for the plant as the man from the museum.

It wasn't actually until the end of the auction that Berenice realized it was the same man. Old people all looked alike to her: they were equalized by time, freed of their individuality by wrinkles. As she was helping Emma Lynn wrap the carnation, the man silently approached her, stroked her hair, and asked:

"So? Still convinced you'll never get married?"

Berenice didn't answer. Emma Lynn looked up and stopped tying the bow that cinched the plant's cellophane wrapping. She locked her eyes on the stranger, but said nothing. Berenice realized it was the same man she had seen in the museum a few weeks earlier, but that time he'd been wearing a smock instead of a suit. She could see that her mother was upset, but the shop was full of people milling around, asking questions, and touching the flowers, so Emma Lynn had to wait until that night to yell at her.

Her mother talked nonstop while they finished cleaning up the shop. She always did that when she was angry, which didn't happen often. When it did, though, she would list the dozens of reasons Berenice deserved to be punished: revealing to their neighbor in apartment five the secret to growing perfect roses, using plastic plates for the cookies instead of ceramic ones, trusting the first stranger she met on the street. The list went on, but Berenice had stopped paying attention. Right then, like in one of those games that show two pictures that look identical but contain subtle differences, she remembered all the times she'd seen the carnation man without realizing it. There had been at least three since the museum. The first was right outside her school: she had seen him reading a newspaper in the café across the street as she passed by with a few classmates, deciding whether or not to head down to the river. A few days later, she'd felt his gaze through the window of Max Cercone's barbershop. And there was a third time, at Ship of Fools. That time, the man had sat silently with a cup of tea and a book while she talked with Halley about Emma Lynn's plans for the auction.

That night, Berenice let her mother list mistakes dating all the way back to the previous summer, and accepted her punishment (no visits to Omar and Halley for a week, organizing all the closets in the house) without complaint. She'd only told Emma Lynn about the encounter she'd had with the man at

the Museum of Art and Natural History. She didn't want to
know what punishment her mother would come up with if she
confessed what she'd just realized: that the carnation man had
been following her, and had probably only come to the auction
because she, Berenice, had accidentally told him about it.

6

There were only five keys in the box that could fit such a small lock.

The first one had the virtue of shutting her up. Vik was surprised by the physical signs of his pleasure (salivation, a slight dizziness) at her silence, which was clearly an indication of panic.

The second key went halfway into the lock, but it made her drag herself to the farthest reaches of her thirty-square-foot kingdom. More silence with the third. It was the fourth that produced a triumphant click. Vik turned the knob and opened the door, his arm following its full arc. He pressed his weight into his cane and stepped back, like someone contemplating a landscape.

"It's over," he said in his language. "I'm not going to hurt you" would have been more appropriate, or at least more cinematic, but he wasn't in a position to make promises.

One of the boxes on the bottom shelf moved, and in the darkness composed of shopping bags and piles of discarded clothes, he saw the outline of a heap. The smell of urine pushed him back another step. His eyes searched for the bucket. He found it in the corner, half hidden between two piles of newspapers. It wasn't red. It was yellow, with a pink star in the middle, one of those toy buckets children use for making sand castles. He quickly detected two other things that didn't belong to him: a gym bag in one corner and, on one of the shelves, with a blanket tossed over them, two plastic jugs that seemed to be full of water.

He addressed her again. This time in her language. Nothing. She apparently had no intention of making his job any easier. Was she waiting for him to go in there and drag her out?

Looking at the heap, he tried to reconstruct the female form he'd seen through the surveillance camera. Only the white dress made it possible. But what if he was wrong? If that wasn't a woman in front of him? He had invested time and energy on the basis of that certainty and the thought of any other possibility made his heart race. He took two steps into the closet, holding his breath to delay his encounter with the smell (which, again, wasn't only of urine—there were plants and fungi, too, clinging to that ammoniac base). With the help of his cane, he kneeled to bring his eyes level with the second shelf.

Once his eyes adjusted to the darkness in the closet, he could see that she was lying almost exactly as he'd imagined her: in the fetal position, facing the wall, almost invisible except for the bottom of one of her feet (the other, positioned in front, was lost in the shadows). The only things between them were a few blankets and two suitcases that had probably been her camouflage over the past few days.

Her hair would have been the logical choice. But he only realized that later, when he was already on the floor with her on top of him and his back shattered into multiple nodes of pain. He'd chosen her foot. It was irresistible, so small and so surprisingly pale. Without really thinking about it, he'd reached out and closed his hand around the hardened pad of her heel. She reacted immediately. Making no noise beside the sound of her accelerated breathing, she folded back on herself and knocked him over in a single movement.

Vik had no time to think about the strength of the legs closing around his chest or the agility with which she moved. The two of them rolled around in a pile of smells and unexpected grazes until they found themselves outside the closet. She'd immobilized his arms in just a few seconds and now, sitting on his chest and leaning forward just far enough to hold his wrists down, she looked at him with a trace of confusion, as if deciding what to do with him.

The camera hadn't lied. She was practically a dwarf. Her face was round, with big dark eyes and luminous white skin, pink in places. Her hands felt slick, like she'd just emerged from a dream or a dip in something aquatic or sticky. In contrast to her eyes, her mouth and upturned nose were exaggeratedly small. It was hard to calculate her age. If it weren't for her skin, her breasts, and her strength, she could have passed for a child.

Vik stopped struggling. His cane, which had been his only advantage, was still in the closet and the only way to control the pain in his back was to try and relax. He calculated that if she sensed his passivity and loosened her grip a bit, he could drag himself to the bedroom and take an analgesic (the patch on his arm didn't seem to have any more relief to give). That would give her time to gather her things and get out. He thought it was the most convenient solution for both of them. The most elegant. All he wanted was for her to leave. That, and the wave of silence the pain reliever promised.

The woman released his wrists and leapt to her feet. The tangle of hair settled over her back. Vik had no time to move or adjust the plan he'd just formulated before she'd spun around, yanked the key from the lock, and returned to the closet. The next thing he heard was the definitive click of the latch.

He lay on the floor for a few seconds longer, trying to understand what had just happened. She was obviously not inclined to give up the territory she'd claimed. Much less so now that she'd confirmed the weakness of his organism. Maybe she'd already known it by watching him for days, anticipating an easy victory.

Grabbing whatever he could reach of the furniture and trying to keep anything from touching his back, Vik dragged himself to the bedroom. The bottle of pills was on his nightstand. He took one with the last sip of water left in his glass and lay down on the bed. A few minutes later he was asleep, but not before thinking (with the last of his strength transfigured into paranoia) what a perfect victim he'd make, in the event that the woman in the closet decided to strangle him or shatter his skull with any of the many objects that inconveniently decorated his room (the pedestal lamp, the stone totem, one of the heavy bronze owls steadying the row of books on his desk).

∞

He still had some of his old way with words. If a gal knew how to listen, underneath those apocalyptic predictions, those invented or confused names (I listened with horror as he said "Bridgend" like it was a person), beyond the almost religious tone of warnings about the dangers of altering the natural order, underneath his incoherent declarations about animal madness ("the mark of an intelligence that evolved over the past forty years for the sole purpose of destroying us"), aside from all that, fighting against the tangle of antipoetic discoveries that the disease put in his mouth, there it was, clear as day, the voice of Frank Smithfield, alias Francisco, one of the leaders of that commune of exceptional beings no one remembers anymore.

But that was a long time ago. Before Gutierrez traveled the world to collect mushrooms and plants. It was a different era, one you could believe in. The way you believe in a sunbeam or a storm. The solid, pure gold of days without night. That's what we were going to be. Maybe what we were. Until Gutierrez and the rest of them got interested in entheogens and the wisdom of all those cultures sacrificed at the altar of plastic and electricity. I'm curious. Isn't that the rule? Surrender to the bigger animal or disappear? Thing is, they didn't think so. They were the ones who started all that nonsense about a return to the woods, or—according to them—a return to a higher state of consciousness. And there was Gabi, to be their perfect emissary.

Of course they were all in love with her. Of course they'd all had a piece of her. That was never the question. Gabi gave out her body like exquisite alms she'd never had to fight for. With joy and a little surprise at having it all, such divine tits and ass. We ladies sensed it, too. I won't say we admired her. No. We accepted her. The age difference saved me, at least, from comparison and competition. Or so I thought.

I remember that day, the one time we went into town together. Someone decided we needed butter. Do you realize what that means? A person's life can change forever because another person needs butter. The kitchen was a disaster that day; it looked like it had been ransacked by an army. Stacks of dirty plates, eggshells, and empty cans piling up in one corner. A few ice trays and a bottle of hot sauce in the fridge. There was nothing in the cabinets but a bag of flour, a bottle of vinegar, and a bag of apples we'd bought from some local farmers (our vegetable garden had been a failure: the only crop that had taken was some bitter fava beans we'd gotten sick of eating). Our money and our plans to get more had run out a while back. Working wasn't an option. Gutierrez was traveling; Clarke, locked in the basement watching silent movies with some girls. Frank and the musicians on shift were practicing in the dining room (the poor thing had "learned" to play the kettledrum on one of the trips he'd taken with Gutierrez; I think the others either put up with it or were too drugged out to notice he had no talent). I was hungry. Back then, I was always eating something. My hunger was existential, colossal, yawning.

From his spot on the threadbare carpet, a young man with large amber-colored eyes said he knew a recipe for apple pie that only took flour and butter. Gabi was sprawled on a sofa with three of her admirers, two girls and a guy with a bald head and a red beard who was a little older and called himself an artist. Since he arrived, he'd spent his time filling droppers of different sizes with paint, which at some point he'd sprinkle over a piece of wood the size of one of the living room walls. He called it "Cosmic Syllabification." Imagine. The point is, Gabi looked up at me from that human mass, untangled her arms and legs, and said, "Come on, Berilia, let's go spread some magic. And buy butter."

You had to climb two hills to get to the nearest store, which was in a gas station. They didn't like us in town. It took a lot of guts to walk into Mrs. Briggs's shop and face that line of serious expressions. After the episode with the police and the underage boy, we tried not to attract too much attention. In the name of freedom and of Gutierrez and Clarke's experiments, we'd always take the longer, less traveled way to the gas station, or else we'd pile into a van and go to another town, where our peculiarity would get lost among the tourists.

So we headed out. Me and Gabi. For butter. Like two little girls in a fairy tale. She wanted to bring Leo, the dog she always had with her, but I wouldn't let her: they hated us enough already, without our bringing a dog into their store. I remember the two of us walked like we were inside a ray of sunlight. She'd already become the favorite. Not for being pretty, though. A few months earlier, she'd figured out how to grow albaria. Others had tried it before and failed; they hadn't even managed to get the seeds to germinate. How could they have? They were just a bunch of kids who wanted to get high.

But Gabi didn't give up. She'd been researching the flower since that one time we tried it. Frank, a guy named Tony (another one from the "old guard"), Gabi, and I were the ones Gutierrez chose for the session. It rained that day. No matter how hard I try, I know I'll never fully be able to put that trip into words. This wouldn't be my first attempt. The only thing that comes close is what I said before about the suppression of time and language. Yeah. That. I remember feeling like a viscous, simple universe all closed in on itself. Like a wise, motionless snake. That's how I felt. Frank, Gabi, and all the bodies around me disappeared, transformed into sources of sounds and odors. Sources of heat and worry, more than anything. Yeah. A blind, absolute, paralyzing wisdom. That's how I'd describe albaria.

Gutierrez had questioned the locals, but no one in the islands had known or wanted to reveal the secrets of the seeds. He didn't care: he had a long list of substances he wanted to experiment with. After our session, though, Gabi took over. It was strange to see her throw herself into a task. She abandoned her meditation technique and her followers. For a little while, she even acted like a "healthy" young woman. She'd disappear in the mornings, hitchhike to campus, and spend the day in the library. She also visited the nurseries in the area. That was around when she adopted the deer. A young buck, practically a fawn, that Clarke found starving to death by the side of the road. Its mother had been hit by a car. Gabi brought it home and it lived with us for a while, like another resident. When it got too big, we built an enclosure in the garden. Gabi fed it every morning and spent hours on end brushing its coat. The whole thing always seemed to me like another one of her extravagances, another attempt by a desperate girl to assert her difference.

But we were talking about the day we went to town for butter. It was hot, and neither of us was wearing a hat. I remember how the sun felt. "Like a halo," Gabi declared, and started in on one of her speeches about energy and the breath. Like I said, she had a tendency to preach, and her words made my hunger and my hangover worse; I felt like I was carrying the whole sun on my head. A forty-something-year-old woman with copper hair pulled her yellow car up to us and asked if we needed a ride to town. Without consulting me, Gabi said yes and opened the back door. I sat in the front. I heard her laugh and ask the woman to turn on the radio. The woman looked at her in the rearview mirror. There was tenderness in her eyes. When she turned to look at me, on the other hand, they went hard as coal.

Gabi started filing a broken nail with the leather strap of her purse. There were no trees on that stretch of road and it was five or six degrees hotter in the car. The whole thing, us three and the yellow car, felt to me like a mirage wrapped in a bubble of heat. One of Bob Dylan's drowsier songs was playing on the radio, which made the sensation even more intense. I heard Gabi ask the woman if she had any nail polish. She looked startled. She said no, but if we went to her friend's apartment with her, she could get some for us. And whatever else we wanted. She asked Gabi if she was hungry. Gabi said yes. That she'd been dying for a hamburger and a Coke. Then she added:

"It's your nails, where you really see how the fetus is consuming you. I must need more calcium. Or iron. One of those things. I'm sure it's going to be a boy. They're more fragile than girls. They need more care."

That was when I saw what the woman driving the yellow car saw. Not two girls walking to town, wrapped in a sunbeam. She saw a brunette in jeans that were too tight for her and a top that announced she was in denial of not being a teenager anymore, and a skinny black girl with puffy eyes in a green gauze dress that just barely covered the bump of a baby she'd been carrying for months. I was obviously dragging Gabi along with me on the road to ruin, rather than the nearest town. That's why she'd stopped. That's why she was trying to take us to her friend's apartment. Blessed be the middle class, so easily scandalized, with their yellow cars, their tooth whitening, and their French manicures. Blessed be vacations paid in installments. Blessed be money well spent on Pyrex, Prozac, and psychologists.

I'm not sure if anyone at Bridgend knew. I think Gabi came up with this excursion because she wanted my complicity. She wanted to get rid of the baby. I hated her for that. For putting me above her in such an obvious way, like I was her mother or some spinster aunt. But she got it. My complicity, I mean. Which isn't saying much. My tears, my words, my complicity, they aren't worth a thing. Make sure you write that down, Doctor. It's what a person does that matters in the end. What she does. Sure, Gabi could count on me, but not to get rid of the baby: now that we had a real chance to prove that the community worked, that there was another way, that we didn't all need to fall for the biggest lie, I wasn't about to let some damned irresponsible girl ruin it.

Because the next thing she did, right there in the car, was run through a list of all the substances she'd taken over the past few months. I saw the woman's hands tighten on the wheel. I saw her eyes, which had been hard as coals, burn with indignation. I saw her weighing options and anticipating reactions. That woman didn't deserve the life running through her veins. Her skin was so white you could see her blood passing dazed through a body that had never shaken with pleasure or hit a high note off-key, much less ridden life at a gallop. In the back seat, Gabi had begun to cry. She was saying that she was afraid the baby would be born a monster. That he'd be deformed, that all those drugs were bound to have consequences and that maybe it was her punishment for not knowing who the father was. That the baby was the child of all the men she'd slept with since arriving at Bridgend. I thought it was fantastic, and couldn't believe that she didn't understand what it meant. An entirely communal child, one hundred percent. Just imagine.

I don't know which was worse, the woman driving with her arms stiff and her back too straight, or the girl soaked in tears and terrified of her own body. Fact. Beauty never made anyone stronger. No matter how much of it Gabi had, she was always going to be that defenseless little animal in the back seat of a stranger's car. She was about two minutes away from asking the woman to adopt her. And the woman, please. She was practically calling her "my child" like those fake mothers in stories.

The woman reached for the dashboard lighter. She'd stuck a cigarette between her lips. I watched her fix herself up as she talked. She was trying to buy time. She was probably trying to calculate Gabi's age. Yeah, she must have thought Gabi was a minor. She must have thought she could go to the police. I felt her thinking it with a clarity I haven't known in years.

All I had to do was lift my left hand and hit her quick with the back of my fist. Yeah, this fist, just as effective back then as it is now. My knuckles got her right in the nose. My other hand went straight for the wheel. I think she instinctively put her foot on the brake because the car came to a stop silently, majestically.

The woman's face was covered in blood. The cigarette had fallen into her lap and had burned a hole in her salmon-colored dress. Gabi had thrown herself on the floor and was screaming for me to stop, that it was bad karma, that I was crazy. Stuff like that. I got out, opened the back door, and dragged her out of the car. Then I went back, opened the white leather purse that had been on the dashboard the whole time, took all the money out, and stuck it in my pocket with the car keys. The woman had her hands over her face and was crying. Making a noise like she had the hiccups. I grabbed her by the hair and banged her head against the window a few times until she stopped.

"No one," I said to Gabi as she sat on the asphalt and cried, "no one is going to come rescue you. Time to get cleaned up and buy some butter."

And that's how we left the highway and walked to town with a new complicity between us. And how that night in Bridgend we all ate, on top of the apple pie, ribs and corn-bread and a bunch of other treats the community celebrated without questioning even once how I'd been able to multiply a few coins into a feast straight out of the movies. (No one asks where something came from if it came free.)

Gabi ate in silence, happier than she'd been in days. Or at least it seemed like that to me. Fact: there's no better form of domination than sharing a crime or a cause for shame. From that moment on, the woman in the yellow car brought us together with just as much force as the baby growing with every bite in the belly of that irresponsible and ill-fated girl with a brain fried by religious pamphlets and pseudoscientific magazines.

☙

Berenice had a very clear picture of the people who called themselves dropouts. She imagined them naked, dirty, and muscular, living in tents pitched in a clearing in the woods, where it was always summer, or sitting around a campfire in a cloud of smoke. The water game also appeared in that image (in the form of a waterfall cascading into a lake), which disturbed her. So did the carnation man, wearing a suit and gazing seriously at the group, which he belonged to in a mysterious way that not even Berenice could explain. But no matter how hard she tried, she couldn't imagine Emma Lynn among them, with her beautiful dresses, her complicated beauty routine, and her perfect curls—which she sometimes wore in an old-fashioned style, gathered in a ribbon at the crown of her head to accentuate her features, while falling loose across her lovely back. Berenice thought it was much more likely that she'd run off with a man, a threat she made often, especially when Berenice insisted on asking about her father.

Emma Lynn's account of the circumstances surrounding her birth never changed: "When I felt like I was running out of time to have a beautiful baby girl, I went to a bar and found the handsomest man there. I slept with him and nine months later, my wish came true." More than the story, the different faces her mother made while telling it stuck with Berenice. In her memories, as she spoke Emma Lynn had her hands in a flower-pot or was spreading liquid mud on her face, one of the oldest beauty tricks in the book. Then she would add, returning to the story, "It's surprisingly easy, I could do it again. The trick is to not get caught up in the fantasy of love. I mean, of course I could still fall in love, lots of people insist on it, but then you'd end up alone, and we don't want that, do we?"

That time they were in the bedroom and Emma Lynn was talking to Berenice in the mirror. She'd made a point of look-ing her in the eyes when she said the word "alone," as she fin-ished doing Berenice's hair in dozens of Medusa braids, as she always called them. "Go on, time to turn those boys to stone," she'd said, giving her a pat on the bottom. And Berenice had left for school feeling like she had superpowers, like she had a vast, vegetal force safeguarding her. Because even though her mother had explained the Greek myth to her, Berenice was convinced that "medusa" was the name of a plant; what a waste that would be, if not. She'd find it one day, she promised herself, and it would be magical. The medusa would be able to detect evil in people's faces. A girl could save a lot of time with a plant-based potion to help her tell who was good and who was bad.

The carnation man, for example, was one of those who complicated her life. She couldn't tell if he was good or bad. From the moment she saw him months earlier, during her school field trip to the natural history museum, the man had hung in her mind, awaiting her verdict. The fact that he'd fol-lowed her afterward and then showed up at the auction didn't make it any easier for Berenice to decide.

The reason for the field trip was to see the exhibition of life-sized dinosaurs, dolls made of iron and latex accompanied by interactive machines that told their story and explained their extinction. You could press a button to get the characteristics and habitat of each specimen and learn who used to eat whom, which was the best part of the whole show.

Berenice got bored right away and broke off from the rest of the group. She passed through savannas and tropical jungles with howler monkeys and birds that, with the flapping of their wings and their cawing, silenced a family of four. They were squeezed onto a bench facing a display in which a leopard stalked a herd of antelope. Berenice preferred the sounds of the jungle to the succession of silent prehistoric giants she'd just left behind. In the African wing, she was surprised by the diorama of an Arab mailman being attacked by lions. The man had managed to kill one of them, but the second had already clawed a deep gash into his camel's leg and, climbing up the animal's flank, was going straight for the throat of the driver, who faced it with a small and not particularly intimidating saber. Did he survive? Berenice hoped not. It would be more fair for the lions to win than for them to be sacrificed so someone in London or Bombay could get their letters on time.

In the mountains, she stood in front of the bears for a long time. She could hear water flowing and the wind in the pines. A female and her cub had stopped to drink from a stream. Farther off, hidden behind some rocks, a large, dark male watched them with fire in his eyes. The female had been preserved in the act of baring her teeth at him. The sign next to the glass read: "The male is an unwelcome presence in this intimate scene." Berenice agreed. Even if the fat brown bear was the cub's father, he looked like nothing but trouble. In fact, he looked like he had every intention of eating his offspring.

Those rooms were practically empty, so she could spend all the time she wanted listening to the animals. She kept going, hoping to find more theatrical taxidermy. But when she reached the third floor, she came across a dark room full of human figures. She realized she was walking through ice, because it was actually colder in that part of the museum and the blocks felt real to the touch. It was like entering an underground castle or a frozen labyrinth where everything glowed pale blue without ever reaching white. She was in a country where the residents hung clothing and canoes from their domed ceilings; in one corner, they'd built a fire and a few fish were cooking for all eternity; in another, one of them had left a blanket half woven. Until the inhabitants finally appeared, armed with spears and covered in pelts, hunting seals or tossing snow in one another's face, children and adults mixed up in laughter that the wind enveloped in hard and distant gusts.

Then came the woman with the bowl in her lap. She seemed to be cooking something. She lived in a tiny hut that was even darker than the rest, and she sang the same phrase over and over. But what really caught Berenice's attention, what she'd remember from that trip to the museum, was the next display. The one with the saddest bride in the world.

She was very young, with big eyes, and her long hair was divided into two braids that had been adorned with flowers for the ceremony. She had clearly been baking, because her face had streaks of flour on it. She was wearing earrings made of cotton, and a short white dress, and she was carrying a tray with an ear of corn on it. The other characters seemed to be chasing her more than they were accompanying her. It looked like they wanted to take something from her, probably the corn, since she was carrying the tray at the height of the visitors' arms, as if she had no other choice but to entrust them with the protection of her weighty load. Come to think of it, Berenice reasoned, they all looked really sad: the man with the dead pig slung over his shoulder, the groom hiding behind dark glasses, and even the little boy, who was frozen in the act of playing with a piglet he led around by a rope. If the sign next to the display hadn't told her it was a wedding, Berenice would have thought someone had died.

That's what she was thinking about when she saw, reflected in the glass, a man in a beige smock appear behind her.

"People think they're our ancestors, but they're really us," he said.

"Us? Who?" asked Berenice, looking up in confusion, because the man (someone she obviously had nothing in common with, since he was old, very white, and tall) wasn't even looking at her, he was looking at the display.

"Mhm." He lowered his eyes to her as if it was hard for him to break the spell of his dolls. "All of us, I suppose. All of us who live here, I mean."

"I hope at least I won't have to be kneading bread until the last minute on my wedding day."

The man laughed and explained that the Comalli revered corn, and that the flour on the bride's face was actually sacred makeup.

"Just like the blush your mother probably uses," he added. "We're alike in that way, too. Always trying to improve ourselves, perfect ourselves." He stretched his arm out across the entire display, and when he spoke again it was louder and more slowly. "Always getting married and unmarried. Must be exhausting, don't you think?"

"I don't know. I don't want to get married."

"Neither does he," the man said, pointing to the boy with the piglet. "But one day, he will. There's no getting around it."

Berenice wanted to ask him why they had to follow in the footsteps of the Comalli and not of the ice people, who seemed happy, playing in the snow with their fishing poles. But maybe, she thought, happiness has to do with the weather, with being close to the Arctic Circle. Then she pointed to the next display, which appeared after a curve, at the end of the hall. Inside there were two men nearly hidden behind some trees, facing away from the visitor and toward the light, as if they were about to walk through the wall, which was illuminated from the floor up. One of the men was missing an arm. The other had the head of a deer.

"And those guys? Why aren't we like them?"

The man looked down with the blank stare of someone leaving a football game or a movie, still totally immersed in what they just witnessed.

"Because it's not possible. The ones who tried only ended up hurting themselves."

Just then, the elevator door opened and another employee in a beige smock walked over, supporting his weight on a cane. He stopped a few paces from them and coughed gently.

"Ah, Vik," said the old man, and walked over to read something the newcomer held out in a folder.

Berenice seized the chance to scurry downstairs. She would have liked to have seen the deer man up close, but it was getting late and her teachers were probably looking for her. Also, she was worried the man might start talking to her again. She'd never met anyone who talked like him.

Not long after that, the same man had waited for her outside her school, found out the address of the flower shop, showed up at the auction, and bought the *Gloria artificialis*. On top of that, since the auction he'd been calling her mother all the time and sending her postcards.

7

He woke at ten thirty from a brief, uneventful sleep. It was snowing. Without sitting up, he checked and confirmed that the pain was still there, like a song that reveals its complexity when played at a low volume. His body was covered in a layer of sweat that became a new source of irritation each time he brushed against himself. A shower, a light lunch, and work on the Ploucquet were calling. He calculated that he had at least four good hours left in him before his body fell apart again. He couldn't afford any more distractions.

Before heading down to the basement, he prepared a tray with a cheese sandwich, grapes, and yogurt and left it on the floor in front of the closet. He meditated for a moment on the best way to let the woman know it was there. In the end, he banged on the door and shouted, "Food!" feeling more like a butler than a warden.

He worked on Romeo's arm for half an hour. It was important to finish that phase of the restoration, clean the limb thoroughly, and restuff it in the same day. The task was complicated by the fact that he had to maneuver the loupe, the needle, and the filling all at once. The animal's paw was in such a state of deterioration that it nearly fell apart between his fingers. He considered inserting a plastic or wood support, now that every size and position imaginable could be ordered from a catalog. But that would have been like tossing the Ploucquet in the incinerator. No. He needed to make do with the same materials dear Hermann would have used in 1851.

At eleven, he thought he heard the creak of the door to the closet or of the wooden floor. He imagined the woman creeping over to the tray, sniffing the food before bringing it to her mouth, eventually nibbling a corner of the bread and accepting, simultaneously, both the danger and the gift. Vik set his tools on the table, reached out, and took a sip of the mint tea getting cold at his side. He looked around. The workshop was full of potential poisons; it would be easy for him to find the right one. By that point, he wasn't even surprised by the thought: he had to consider every option. He was certain she was doing the same thing, two floors up.

He couldn't resist the temptation to check his phone. No. She hadn't crept anywhere or sniffed the food. She'd opened the closet door wide, set the tray on her lap, and was now leaning against the doorframe, eating grapes. The camera wasn't able to capture her movements in detail, but it looked like she was even removing their skins before popping them into her mouth.

He finished his tea in a single gulp and went back to work. But he couldn't shake her. He felt her closing in on him behind the forced regularity of his movements. His needle and pliers would waver, the stuffing would come out again, and he'd have to start over. First, she was one of the many victims of the hurricanes that were buffeting the country and sending a wave of people northward. Like him, she'd lost everything and was walking barefoot and disoriented through an unfamiliar city. They had found one another. He didn't walk with a cane, of course, so nothing impeded their embrace. But the street was filling with other refugees who were walking toward him with unsteady steps and hair full of ash. Hands grabbed at the sleeves of his suit. Then he was standing in front of a soldier from the Coloma army, who was handing him a blanket and cans of food, and she had been lost in the crowd.

After that, she was a housewife with a hardworking husband and three kids, a tortured soul with some hidden talent (he'd bet she painted beautiful watercolors), who had suddenly felt life hanging too heavy on her and decided to get away. She went here and there, flagging down cars on the motorway and panhandling outside women's bathrooms. One day she turned up at the museum—with the naïve hope of showing her watercolors, which she carried in a portfolio under her arm—just as he was walking down the front stairs at closing time. She was wearing a black dress. The top buttons were open to reveal the curve of her breasts, but their exchange dissipated just as he approached her. There were too many pigeons pecking at the stairs (no one knew who'd had the great idea to spread crumbs all over the museum steps, probably the same comedian who put scarves and hats on the *Diplodocus* statue)—all of which decided to take flight at that exact moment, as if they'd agreed in advance. They were indeed pests; he had to give Miss Beryl that. And to top it off, two school groups were barreling out of the building after the last guided tour—which was unavoidable, he supposed, because if he was leaving, that meant it was five o'clock and everyone needed to clear out of the museum, and therefore he really had no other choice but to return to the easiest, the most effective, and also the most plausible option and stick her in one of the many abandoned

houses along Grandville, lying on a mattress with other bodies, young people with blank stares who shared syringes and
spit. Of course she sold herself, indifferently and for pennies.
Of course she wasn't wearing a nightgown but a pair of tight
jeans and a T-shirt that revealed her navel. One day she decided
to leave it all behind. But her willpower only took her as far
as the café across the street, where she collapsed. Then he
appeared. He leaned toward her, swept the hair from her face,
and found her beautiful. He offered his arm and walked her
to his home, straight to his bedroom, to the bed (which was,
strangely, already dirty and unmade), where she did what she
used to do back at the house full of addicts. But now she did
it with a sense of gratitude and with such complete surrender
that, even in his fantasy, she ended up repelling him and sending him back to his worktable, from which the mice looked
up at him with the eyes of rodents and not of characters in an
Elizabethan drama.

⚭

Smithfield didn't mention any of this when he spoke to the
group of old folks at the community center. He couldn't have,
in the first place, since he didn't know the half of what had
happened the day we went to buy butter and came back with
a feast and the news of a communal baby. But he didn't talk
about community, either, or about Gabi, or about the love he'd
said he felt for me until she showed up. Standing in front of our
group of beginners, he talked about deer overpopulation and
misguided youth.

He convinced them. Not with his words, though. With his
urgency. And with the only "argument" he was able to make:
the possibility that deer in the area were going crazy because

of a virus that they in turn brought into the city via their natural parasites. In fact, he said, it was possible that those confused kids living out in the woods were victims of the same disease.

He didn't mention that we'd chased the natural life, too. That we'd believed in similar things, that we'd searched for those other states of consciousness, just like the dropouts, or that we'd failed. He talked about cases of madness in animals. About the sheep that committed suicide in Turkey, the time it rained frogs in Kansas, the zombie pigeons in Ukraine. About the epidemics and the pilgrimages of the Middle Ages. (History always lends a hand when it comes to persuasion.) He passed around photographs and newspaper clippings. It was time to do something, he said, to take back our rightful place in a city where authorities refused to do anything to really guide youth and correct the imbalance that all of us, at the end of the day, had helped create.

It was our duty, he concluded, to act. We had nothing to lose; there were no more sunny corners left in the south where we could retreat with a clear conscience. For a minute, I thought he was talking about those ocean view condos sold to retirees in low-interest installments, but then I realized that maybe he was talking about the Primevals, who were still alive and well in his mind, founding cities along the coastline of the entire continent.

Max Cercone asked why the authorities didn't intervene, why they were still protecting the animals if they'd become a danger to humans. And how was it possible that there was a virus or parasite in our woods and no one knew about it.

"What authorities?" asked Elizabeth Duda, punctuating her words by removing the glasses she'd been using to pretend to read an article written in German about a dog that had tried to kill itself three times in the same lake.

"They're obviously in on it," agreed Heather, massaging her left leg.

"That's right," her sister interjected. "They've never lifted a finger to protect us. Take a look at how the mayor parades around that chubby brat he just adopted."

"I wouldn't be surprised to hear they've already made some secret deal with that band of lunatics. Maybe they're poisoning us and we don't even know it."

"Someone has to be the voice of reason in these crazy times. Have you ever asked yourselves why the community center is run by foreigners? Doctors coming from Serbia, professors arriving from Cuba from one day to the next. Very suspicious. When my wife here and I were in Haiti, we saw all kinds of strange things."

"I've always believed in obligatory cannibalism. If people were forced to eat what they kill, that would be the end of war."

Leaning against the doorframe, Emilia Bourdette tossed out the phrase casually, as if she'd been talking about her preference for cotton clothing. She'd finished out her sentence at the zoo a few days earlier, which apparently gave her the impression she was in a position to revive old slogans that didn't shock anyone, anymore. It's true, her energy was totally different from what we'd seen that day in the gazebo. She walked over to Smithfield, who had turned in his chair and fixed his eyes on the window that was letting in the homogenous gray that was common around these parts. Emilia rested a hand on his shoulder, also casually, like it was a toad or some other pest that had jumped out of her pocket of its own free will. Now that her moment in the spotlight was over, she wore jeans, a straw hat that was definitely out of season, and gardening boots.

She went on:

"The destruction of a harmful system is an act of love. We can do it," she said, then paused and made a fist like an actress in a Golden Age movie. She counted two seconds and added, "Because we're free. We're beautiful." Another pause, and now at the top of her lungs: "And we have all the answers!"

I looked at our audience. The only one who hadn't spoken was Betty Paz (she was obviously asleep behind her dark glasses). I also saw myself, sitting between Smithfield and the Armstrong sisters. Being Beryl Hope. Period. Beryl Herminia Hope, occupying a space where she wasn't anymore, being something undefined or undefinable. A little more, but also a little less, than a wayward old lady.

I saw it in their faces (I saw it in mine) with total clarity. They didn't care whether it was Christ or Buddha, deer or the dopers in the woods. Smithfield's speculations only reached as far as a blind spot in their minds, where they crashed into which pills to take at one forty-five, competed with plans for lunch at Ritter's the next day, and then finally decayed alongside the memory of cauterized veins on an inner thigh, kinesiology sessions, the smell of onion under fingernails (so hard to get out!), and daily exercises to help guide pen over paper without ending up with something that looks like an echocardiogram. If Smithfield had said it was extraterrestrials making the deer crazy, they would have believed him. There was something flexible, malleable in their faces, a force on the verge of exploding. They were tired, they were fed up. All they wanted was to shoot something.

☞

Berenice could tell when it was him because, instead of indulging in one of her monologues that always ended up baffling and persuading her interlocutor, Emma Lynn spoke to him in a voice that was soft and obedient, and there were long silences in their conversations when he, the carnation man, was the one persuading her. Or at least trying to. Because there was a controlled rage in the calm way her mother took in the stranger's words. When she hung up, she stood there looking at the phone for a few seconds, as if she was amazed that the words could reach her through that cable, or as if the object had been a participant in the long argument. Berenice had come to the conclusion that the carnation man wasn't interested in flowers, that he hadn't paid all that money for the carnation because he admired it, but because he wanted to get close to her mother.

The old man had come to the flower shop one other time, a few days after the auction. Berenice was in the back room, in the nursery, watching Purple Queen. It looked like the plant had sprouted a bud that week, something Emma Lynn had thought was impossible. Berenice had kept a close eye on it ever since she discovered the bump crowning one of its branches. She wondered whether the flower would smell the same as the bigger version. She imagined it wouldn't. She imagined that its diminutive size would make it unique.

Emma Lynn was nervous that day. She was expecting the carnation man and had told Berenice she wasn't allowed to leave the nursery until their meeting had ended. A useless precaution, because anyone could have heard their conversation through the glass doors. It was just that Berenice hadn't thought they were saying anything important enough to merit listening in.

The visit had been brief, and Berenice remembered a few snippets of their conversation. The man walked around the flower shop, admiring Emma's most successful grafts and entertaining himself with questions about the names and descriptions of the bouquets in the catalog. After a while, he asked to see the nursery. Emma said no. He asked if she had any orchids. She answered that she planned to try growing tigre tikka from Bolivia, a species almost completely unknown in the north. She preferred, she said, the more modest versions of those flowers and not the laboratory-produced specimens that husbands bought for their wives to make up for too many years of cohabitation. There was something perverse in that whole industry of compensation, Emma said. She didn't want any part of it.

In the end, the man bought a bouquet of grass lilies and left. Berenice had the feeling that her mother was scared of him, which didn't make sense because he seemed very polite. But the carnation man had done more than just buy flowers that day. She was sure of it, and now she regretted not having strained to hear the whispered conversation they'd had beside the front door to the shop. The same door Berenice had avoided for the past few days and which she decided to continue avoiding. She didn't want to run into Mr. Müller or have him see her through his picture window. Come to think of it, she was surprised that he hadn't appeared at the apartment, asking why the flower shop had been closed for so long.

Taking the dirt path that wound its way up from the woods, Berenice stuck her hand in her pocket to make sure that the keys to the back door were still there. As she caught her breath in preparation for the last leg of the climb, she struggled to retrace Emma's exact actions after the carnation man's first visit. She remembered that she, Berenice, had been playing in the dirt set aside for the orchids and had gotten the sleeves of her blouse dirty. But when she left the nursery, Emma hadn't gotten angry. She hadn't even noticed. She was completely focused on the pages of a notebook with a gray cover that she'd pulled from a green backpack.

Berenice knew whose notebook that was. She'd only ever opened it once: it was full of poems about the future, love, and the cosmos. There were also drawings made in blue ink. She remembered one of a girl with long, curly hair in concentric circles that transformed into flowers, a garden, a duck pond, and deer. The afternoon Emma found her reading it, she sat down next to her and said that the notebook, the canvas backpack, a guitar, and a few photos were all that was left of Gabi, so they needed to be extra careful with them. She explained that the poems were songs, which was why they had those little symbols floating in the lines above the words. Those were musical notes. "I always wanted to learn to play an instrument. Maybe one day I'll ask someone to play these for me. To hear how they sound," Emma had said.

It was hard for Berenice to believe that the slim girl in the photos, with the perfect nose and long, curly hair, was her grandmother. When she asked why they never visited her grave but did visit Great-grandma Cecilia, Emma answered that Gabi had asked to be cremated and that her ashes be scattered in the woods. "She probably figured she'd be everywhere that way. The fool," Emma said, involuntarily clenching her left hand into a fist.

Berenice hadn't seen her look at the notebook again until the afternoon the carnation man came to visit. Hiding her mud-stained hands behind her back, Berenice asked what she was reading.

"I'm not reading. I'm looking," said Emma, turning a photo over in front of her. In it, two women and five men were lined up in front of a house that looked like a castle. They were smiling. One of them was Emma's father and Berenice's grandfather; it's just that no one knew which. Years earlier, when she was young and finding out had seemed worth the trouble, Emma had numbered them with the intention of finding out what had become of them. She'd lost steam at number two, a young man with long hair and thick glasses who was now a bald and vaguely famous film producer she was never able to reach directly.

Berenice had no trouble identifying number four as the carnation man, even though he'd gotten more plump and had fine blond hair back then. His eyes were self-assured as he looked at the camera. Eyes that clearly believed nothing bad could happen within the space of that photo. She'd made her way to the counter and was sitting on a stool across from her mother. Emma picked up the picture, stretched out her arm, and held it to her cheek.

"The truth is that neither of us looks like him. Maybe in the eyes, a little bit. Or your ears. They stick out more than mine," she said, amused, which inspired Berenice to cover them with her hands.

Emma giggled and said she looked like those Chinese monkeys that were supposed to be wise because they didn't want to hear anything about the world. Then she laughed. Hard. Berenice didn't find it funny at all to be compared to a monkey, no matter how wise. She looked around the flower shop for something to shut her mother up. There was the backpack, on the corner of the counter. She jumped off the stool and grabbed it at a run, not realizing that one of the straps was caught on the iron rod that held the roll of paper her mother used for wrapping bouquets. The backpack, which was very old, tore immediately. Something like buttons or candies went flying in the air and Berenice ended up on the floor with a piece of fabric in her hand. The other piece, along with the straps, was still hanging from the iron rod. Emma Lynn screamed something incomprehensible, then ran around the counter at Berenice with the obvious intention of dragging her off by the hair, or at least shaking her. But she stopped halfway, knelt down, and started gathering the seeds (not buttons or candies) that had been hidden in the lining of the bag. Once she'd stowed them in an empty pack of cigarettes, she returned to the notebook. She flipped quickly through the pages until she found one where Gabi had pasted the drawing of a plant that had clearly been torn from an encyclopedia or a botany book. "*Salvia lundiana,*" Berenice read over her mother's shoulder, "more commonly known as *albaria* or sweet dream, is a hallucinogenic flower native to the Caribbean and Central America, where indigenous populations have utilized it in religious ceremonies for more than twelve hundred years. According to popular belief, the consumption of its pungent leaves in a fresh state produces an encounter with the inner animal, which then confers its powers on the initiate."

No matter how many times she went through her mother's notebook, Emma Lynn couldn't find any other reference to albaria, or any hint about how it might be grown. There were a few songs that mentioned "the eye-opening dawn," or "natural light," and "the mystery of mended souls," but nothing that resembled instructions or advice about how to cultivate it.

She'd spent that night reading posts on an internet forum about psychoactive herbs and mushrooms. The plant was a source of controversy: some people maintained that it didn't exist, some that it had been wiped out during the conquest, or that the youths who thought they'd tried it back in the seventies must have gotten their hands on a similar species but not the original salvia that appears in the diary of Kristoffer Lund, a nineteenth-century Danish traveler who was one of the few people to ever describe it in detail.

Pretty much everything she read had been a waste of time, she'd told Berenice the next morning. The people who posted on those forums were more interested in finding places where the plant might still be growing in the wild than they were in how to cultivate it.

"Too bad they're only interested in the plant's effects and hardly anyone bothers to learn about its history."

Nothing like a mystery involving plants (and family, Mr. Müller declared when they shared the discovery with him) to get Emma's gears turning. In just a few days, she had come up with more germination experiments and compiled more information about the flower than all those people on the forums who saw themselves as experts in hallucinogens.

That was one of the things she missed most about her mother: everyone around her (even Mr. Müller, one of the rudest, most sullen people they knew) would get caught up in a wave of enthusiasm that made it impossible not to get involved in her projects. It didn't matter that the albaria experiment had failed. Maybe something like that could explain her disappearance: the discovery of another tricky plant that had taken her out of town for a few days.

But Berenice knew it wasn't a likely scenario. She reached the top of the hill, keeping her eyes on the few remaining houses in that part of the neighborhood. Night had nearly fallen, she was cold, and the hope that had been with her as she left the house had vanished as she took stock of the events after the auction. It was clear that her mother hadn't gone on some "expedition" and that albaria, with its white and probably cursed flowers, was responsible for everything that was happening.

8

At eleven twenty-five he was startled by the sound of water and a banging above his head that told him a tap had been opened. On the screen of his telephone, the closet door was ajar and the woman was disappearing down the hall to the bathroom.

He left his instruments on the table. He felt another kind of sweat, neither hot nor cold, on the tips of his fingers. Without his cane, it took him thirty-eight steps to reach the living room staircase from the basement.

His mind had slipped into counting again. When he thought about it (which wasn't often, only on those rare occasions he "caught" himself doing it), he was unable to reach any conclusions. He couldn't say whether it was an attempt to divide the insignificance of those moments into sequences in order to slow them down or, on the contrary, if his mind was trying to grind them into a straight, neat line of numbers to obliterate them and make space for things that really mattered. He counted his steps without any plan or philosophy, just as he counted the intervals between the cigarette and his mouth, the times his needle pierced the dry skin of an animal, the time it took to boil an egg. He'd read that somewhere in the East there were monks who believed they had a finite number of breaths. They maintained that every human being was born with a certain number of inhalations and exhalations at their disposal. This was why the sages focused on breathing deeply and slowly. They saw laughter, love, and tears for what they were: a senseless waste of air. Vik sometimes wondered if his mind's insistence on counting was somehow similar—an awareness of his mortality. His doctor, on the other hand, saw it as part of his obsessive-compulsive disorder and urged him to abandon this and other rituals.

He could hear the water more clearly from the stairs. It was the sound of the bath being filled to the point of over-flowing. Which meant she hadn't even bothered to close the door (that's how confident she was of having dominated her poor host). Just the thought of it restored his strength and he climbed the twenty-three steps, indifferent to the wood creak-ing under his feet and to the numbers.

He found the dress practically in the staircase. Her knickers were a bit closer to the door. It was an implausible but encour-aging detail. The fact that the woman in his closet still wore undergarments gave him hope that he might be able to reason with her, that she might not be beyond the reach of language.

He leaned against the doorframe, enjoying what would probably be the only time he had the advantage, just as she was getting into the bath. He watched her close the tap with her left hand; with her right, she covered her nose and mouth and then sank into the water. Once again, Vik felt the detail (of plugging her nose) was out of place, as if he were the intruder and was watching a little girl play. The tap dripped out three, four notes. She remained underwater.

The steam from the bath made it hard for him to see, but the woman's body was giving off the same smell that had been floating through the house the past few days. It was then that Vik finally recognized it (actually, that's what he'd been trying to do all morning). Without moving or thinking of a plan, he squinted and let the old desperation so tied to that scent invade him.

The woman in the bathtub didn't smell like soil or leavening or sandalwood. It was albaria. He should have identified the scent earlier, when her body was on top of his, but Vik had resigned himself long ago to the fact that his treatments were stripping him of his sense of smell and taste.

He opened his eyes—still trying to reconcile the old, familiar smell with the unrelentingly foreign order of this house in this country—and immediately saw hers, looking straight ahead at a point in the water. Her gaze was serene, if slightly veiled, like it could deflect any flash that might stimulate it. The straight hair plastered to her head revealed a youth that her skin and the bags under her eyes had hidden. Vik calculated that she couldn't be over thirty. And no, he didn't find her beautiful.

She lifted an arm from the water. She grabbed the soap, rubbed it between her hands, spread the foam over her face, and then slid down until she was submerged again. When she came back up, she said:

"I've always thought the face is the only thing worth washing. The rest can just stay dirty."

He'd gotten so accustomed to the idea that she was mute that the sound of her voice (harmonious, natural) sent a chill up his spine. Thirteen seconds passed, diligently counted. Vik shifted his weight from one leg to the other. Finally, he responded.

"There are clean towels in the bedroom. I'll get you one."

CR

The first two classes were theory. I showed them a video of tracking techniques that I got at the public library and a few diagrams of cervine anatomy. I doubt that any of them will actually hunt a deer. If they do get that far, it's even less likely they'll hit one of the two points that guarantee a quick and painless death for the animal. But it seemed important to give them all the information a professional hunter would have. I didn't need any of that: the woods, and years of hunting with my family, were enough.

My father could track a wounded deer for hours; he was even prepared to sleep outdoors if the animal took too long to choose a spot to die. This is the phase where lots of hunters make a mistake: their impatience gets the best of them and they end up losing their kill. It takes days for a deer with a flesh wound to bleed to death. Some even make a full recovery (my aunt Rose, who lived way up on the mountain, used to see a three-legged doe in her garden all the time). It takes a lot of patience, following an animal without sending it into distress, before and after you shoot. Hitting the target isn't the end of the story, far from it. That's why it's so important to aim for the heart or the lungs. A hunter has to be ready to make decisions quickly, to ask herself every chance she gets: Is it ethical to shoot this target? From this distance? The answer seems to be yes if the shot is within the hunter's and her weapon's capabilities, and above all if the target is one of the animal's vital organs. That's the foundation of the hunter's code of ethics. Heart or lung. They all know it. But in practice, there's no time for questions. Even the most experienced hunters have trouble not catching "buck fever," not falling victim to their own adrenaline.

Just imagine it, you've been posted up in a tree or a ditch for hours; imagine your hands are frozen around your rifle, your eyes are tired from reading bite marks on the leaves of bushes and traces of fur left on tree trunks; imagine your body is a shapeless mass of calculations and cold, when out of nowhere, arbitrary as a revelation, a twelve- or fourteen-point buck steps into the picture. The cold disappears and air enters your nose with a force stronger than anything you've known before, but it's somehow still not enough. Your shortness of breath is so surprising that you gasp to take more in and soon you're panting as if you just ran a sprint. Your palms are sweating and your heart loads and fires a thousand times before your fingers do, while that buck saunters right in front of you, grazing at his leisure, maybe a little disoriented by the wind. It takes a lot of experience not to lose sight of the target at a moment like that. Not many hunters manage to shoot for a vital organ under those circumstances. Especially when it's their first buck. Most of them miss. Or they hit the shoulder or a leg, the two worst targets. The weapon is secondary, I've always said. It's the hunter that makes the difference. It's the hunter who gets put to the test. Can she keep her cool? I'd say the question really is: can she keep still, with an animal she didn't even dare to dream of in the crosshairs?

Not many can. Only the ones who hunt for their own, secret reasons. Like my uncle Ben, my father's younger brother, married to my aunt Rose. He used to hunt sometimes with a bow and arrow; he was one of the first to popularize the technique around here. Said that bow hunting evened the playing field.

I asked him once why he hunted. He'd taken me to his favorite spot, up in the mountains, past the bridge destroyed by the summer floods. It's strange, because it never would have occurred to me to ask my father that. (I guess even a little girl could see that my father hunted out of love, that he enjoyed teaching his children to track and identify signs more than he

enjoyed hunting itself.) Ben looked at me like it was the stupidest question in the world. He squinted his gray eyes until
wrinkles formed at the corners (because he was thirty-five and
acted like the world hung from his every gesture, I thought
wrinkles were attractive). He clenched his jaw and a shadow
fell over his sunburnt face.

"To remind myself I'm alone."

It took me years to understand what he was saying. Back
then I probably replied with something even stupider, like,
"You're not alone, Uncle Ben." I know I put my hand on his
knee. In the silence that followed, I realized that he and I had
crossed some kind of threshold. Clearly uncomfortable, he
stood and gestured at the valley and the city, which trembled
in the afternoon light like a mirage. Then he adjusted his cap
and said it was time to head back.

Ask anyone who calls themself a hunter today why they
do it. They'll say it's to "get outdoors" or "spend time with
friends," or "to land a trophy." Fact. Hunters today don't think
twice before they mist themselves with synthetic piss to attract
bucks, or use illegal weapons, or shoot an animal that's lying
down. They only care about the result. Not many of them
know the pleasure of anticipation (the real reason my father
hunted) or of realizing they're alone in the world, alone in the
woods, where we only have two options: hunter or hunted.

Of course I don't expect anyone in our group to understand. I try to stick to Smithfield's explanations and convince
them we're doing a public service. Even you, Dr. Danko,
would agree with that idea. Anyway, it's not like we're the first.
In Black Chapel, the town council approved an ordinance that
makes it legal to hunt in residential areas to reduce the deer
population. Other towns are still debating the issue, but I'm
pretty sure we won't even need a permit in our case; the woods

around the city are so full of deer it would take an army to get rid of them all.

Emilia doesn't see things that way. She paid me a visit yesterday at the museum. She insisted that the deer had stopped acting crazy at the end of the summer, that the episodes of animal violence were getting less frequent, and that it had obviously just been temporary. I told her I was planning to go on with the project, even if Smithfield was hooked up to a machine. I should talk to the authorities, she suggested, if that was the case. She even offered to act as an intermediary. I asked her if having crushed a fawn's skull put her in a better position for diplomacy than the rest of the group. I watched her gaze grow more intense.

"I have anger issues," she said. "It's important to admit these kinds of things, Beryl dear."

Ever since her "rehabilitation," she's been punctuating her sentences with "dear," "honey," or "sweetheart." Like someone who smacks you and then hides their hand. In this case, she was hoping I was going to admit I had some kind of problem. I have no idea what. I'd already caught her whispering something in Max Cercone's ear during our first marksmanship class. That's why I kicked her out of the group. I told her right there, in the museum. That her participation was no longer required, that no group could tolerate a member who went around sowing doubt. I know her type. Too pretty. And beauty always creates needs. The need for maintenance (how many more years are you willing to keep working for that ass? wouldn't it be better to just let it go?); the need to be worshipped (how many times are you going to debase yourself for that compliment, that gift?). Needs, needs, needs. That's what ends up destroying them. Gabi was like that, in her way. Except she was smarter than Emilia, even in her pseudoreligious

delirium. She could see that the days of her reign were numbered. That the most natural course is toward the common
denominator of ugliness. Fact. Sooner or later we all end up in
Gerontozombie storage.

After the day we walked to town together, Gabi kept checking the papers for a story about the woman in the yellow car.
She never found one. I know because I was looking, too. We
never knew what happened with her. But the memory still
bound us together. That and the pregnancy. For a few months,
we were inseparable. We read parenting magazines, picked out
baby clothes, did breathing exercises. The others got involved,
too: Clarke planned a party to pick the baby's name, Gutierrez
hired a midwife so the birth could be communal and happen
at Bridgend. Frank ran around satisfying any request Gabi or
I would make; he could've written a song, he was so happy.
Yeah, those were months of pure enjoyment. Finally, something was brewing at home, something that promised to be
even bigger than the Big Concert. And that's how Celeste was
born. A perfect little girl who defied all her mother's fears. My
fondest memories of Gutierrez are from those afternoons he
spent with the baby in his arms, shaking pieces of brightly
colored paper to get her to stop crying. And Clarke, the most
reserved among us, who made an effort anyway to make sure
she grew up healthy. Yeah, Celeste was the Big Party. For all of
us except Gabi.

For starters, she was never able to breastfeed. Either the
milk wouldn't come, or she couldn't handle the pressure of
her daughter's mouth. The doctors recommended an outra-
geously expensive formula. Gabi spent her days in the attic
or in a rocking chair with Celeste in her arms and a vacant
look in her eyes. One time she told me that she'd dreamt she

heard the baby crying, and it kept getting louder and louder and she found herself in a big, empty white room full of sunlight, without a single piece of furniture or anywhere someone could hide a baby. She looked everywhere for her, until she finally realized that she was wearing her. Yeah. That's what she said. That she was wearing her, stuck to her belly like a dress. And she'd understood that the baby had been there the whole time, and that she was going to stay right there, crying for both of them, and that there wasn't a song or a balanced meal in the world that could calm her.

It was around then that I decided Gabi, Celeste, and I would take one of the empty bedrooms on the second floor. She was in no condition to take care of her daughter. Another time, Clarke caught her in the van—she was about to leave for the woods because "someone" had warned her that her daughter was in danger at Bridgend.

There are names for that now. You should know them, Doctor. Maybe they would have applied to Gabi. But back then, no one was talking about postpartum depression or psychosis. It's not easy to believe we're just a conglomeration of hormones, that our failures might be the result of a chemical, electrical, or contractual imbalance in our brains. It goes against our idea of what's "natural." Since when is it "natural" for a mother to decide she can't stand her son or daughter? Not so smart for the proliferation of the species, right? On the other hand, some animals kill their offspring. It's true. Pigs, for example: I've read that mothers eat their defective young in an act of population, or misery, control. They're definitely sparing them the humiliation of being different. Back then, though, these thoughts didn't even cross my mind. I believed in everything. That is, I refused to believe in hormones—I thought that above and beyond genes and anatomy there was a self, a redeeming center that would prevail, that would never be left to the mercy of instinct.

Not anymore. Now I'm inclined to admit the opposite. Besides, I was more worried about Celeste than I was about Gabi; to me, her instability was just as much a part of her as the beauty marks on her chest. Yeah. Something was already broken in that little head of hers, which is why none of us paid attention. We were wrong about that, like we were about so many things.

I remember a few of those nights, the two of us talking from one bed to the other, me listening to the sounds coming out of the cradle at the foot of mine. Those were some of the most sincere conversations I had with her. She told me about how she'd known she wasn't going to grow old since she was a little girl. About how she'd trained herself to look without fear at dead things and had come up with a plan not to join them too late.

That might be how we lost paradise. Don't you think? Once we began to anticipate, scrutinize—and, most of all, try to solve—death. What I mean is, that's how we lost the last thing connecting us to the beasts. Real paradise is not knowing, or living as if you didn't. That time, it was Gabi who was wrong. I guess the kind of contemplation she discovered in the religions of India is meant to remind us of our expiration date. Just like certain poems and certain ways of approaching science. A load of crap. I want to know what that anticipation gets you. Better to live your life forgetting it, or thinking you'll be an exception. Yeah, much better to come up with diversionary tactics. Hunting deer is as good as any other. You know it, too, Doctor. That's why you put us in front of this camera. Fine, so the world keeps turning, time for some distraction.

CR

From the outside, the flower shop still looked like an extension of Mr. Müller's house. Inside, though, was a map of Emma Lynn's preferences and whims. The simple, semicircular counter was made of wood. It was too high for Berenice (it had come from a gaunt, melancholy tobacconist who'd watched his clients die off one by one), so she had to sit on a stool to be on the same level as the customers, which made her seem like a security guard; the bouquets of roses and gladiolas lined up in front of it guaranteed that people didn't come too close. The counter was hollow in the back. Emma Lynn had shelves built in, and these quickly filled with boxes of seeds, papers, notebooks, receipts, and books.

To the right of the door, in front of the blue-and-gold stained-glass window, were the bouquet stands. Their arrangement and contents depended on the season and on the mood of Emma Lynn, who occasionally waged secret wars against a few of the local farmers. She'd stopped buying from the one with the best tulips around because he'd dared to offer her Rembrandts grown using a chemical developed in Japan.

To the left, by the red-and-green window, were the trees and plants for sale: bougainvillea, cherry trees, wisteria, potted ivy, and periwinkle alternated by season with firs, ficus plants, poinsettia, morning glory, and elephant ear. Around Christmas, Emma made a special point of getting miniature pines. She would try to convince her customers to adopt living trees for their gardens instead of continuing to decimate the forest in service of their consumerist zeal. Only a few of them took her advice.

The back room was what they called the nursery. It was a simple rectangle closed off on two sides with glass. A door in the far wall opened onto the woods. The slope leading to the cemetery was off to the right; on a clear day, you could even see a few of its more imposing monuments.

The nursery was also where all the tools were kept: spades, scissors, and little syringes were lined up on Emma's worktable; shovels, hoses, rakes, and shears hung from the wall the nursery shared with the shop. The watering cans, in different shapes and sizes, lived on the shelves with the lamps, buckets, and flowerpots. Plants, experiments, and other projects covered four perfectly aligned white wooden benches (also purchased from the church), and, in one corner behind a shoji screen, there was a cot where Emma took increasingly long naps.

A lukewarm air always glided through those two rooms, though it was more like a murmur or an insistence. A stubbornness of branches, buds, and blossoms that felt like an organism preparing itself, a being composed of hundreds of other tiny, insignificant beings convinced they were part of some greater order.

It was into this organism that Berenice stepped on that Friday afternoon. The flowers weren't in catastrophic shape, but there was plenty of room for improvement. Several violets had haloes of exhaustion on their petals, and the dahlias had lost their composure. A few of the chrysanthemums were still in flower and required special care. But before she did any of that, Berenice headed straight for the folding screen, stomping loudly on the cement. If Emma Lynn was hiding there, she was going to get a piece of her mind.

Yes, there was someone on the cot, facing the wall. But it wasn't Emma Lynn. It was Mr. Müller. It took Berenice a few seconds to recognize him. His belly seemed even bigger and his shiny red face looked longer than usual because he was sleeping with his mouth open like a fish, forcing out powerful gusts that never quite became snores, though not for lack of trying.

Her first instinct was to run. But she immediately realized that if he was there, it was because he'd noticed that Emma hadn't opened the shop in days. Maybe he knew something about all this. She shook him gently. Nothing. She tried placing both hands on his left arm and pushing him toward the wall. That didn't do it, either. She changed strategies: standing at the foot of the cot, she grabbed his wrists and pulled until his torso popped up like a doll's. Mr. Müller opened his eyes and said a single word.

"Water."

Berenice went over to the nursery sink and returned with a full glass, which he emptied in one gulp.

"I went looking for you at your house yesterday, but you weren't there," he said. "The Belchers told me they hadn't seen you in days. I'd thought that idiot mother of yours had come back for you. But now I see I was mistaken."

Berenice's eyes filled with tears at the way Mr. Müller said that last part. How could he be more powerful than Connie, Omar, or Halley? None of them had managed to make her cry. That was why she hadn't considered him as a possible relative: he always added an insult on to everything he said. And he licked his lips when he talked, like he was always just finishing lunch. Berenice kept waiting for him to finally pull a napkin from his pocket and wipe his mouth, but that never happened.

Mr. Müller straightened his clothes. He closed the last few buttons of his shirt to cover the bush of white hair growing from his chest, sat more comfortably on the cot, then leaned back against the wall and went on speaking, his words thicker and slower than usual.

Emma Lynn, he said, had been acting strangely since the summer. He'd taken it upon himself to keep an eye on her. "You might not be aware, but I have quite a view. And good windows. I know everything that goes on in this neighborhood." Of course Berenice and her mother knew it. The stained glass wasn't just an aesthetic whim on Emma's part: it also served to hide the details of her business from the gaze of her former employer. The years they'd worked together in the pharmacy had been enough to establish a certain familiarity between them. Or a routine, which is the same thing. Emma would tolerate his rudeness and irritability, and he got to be partially involved in their lives. Keeping his involvement partial was the most challenging aspect of the routine, something that required a considerable investment of Emma Lynn's diplomatic skills. When she got the idea to start producing ointments and growing medicinal plants, Mr. Müller became her involuntary advisor. All it took was a glass of whiskey to get him talking about active ingredients and brain receptors, to transform him from an old man with too much time slipping through his strangely elegant hands into the youth who had studied pharmacology and biochemistry long ago.

Still, Berenice thought, Mr. Müller wasn't as innocent as he seemed. To start with, the whiskey hadn't clouded his mind at all while he was participating in these projects. He remembered every detail of his conversations with Emma, and—though he certainly did want things to go well for his tenant—there was something fishy about his involvement with the albaria project. When Emma transplanted her only specimen to a flowerpot, he'd started researching its effects. He was the one who arrived at the flower shop one day with a book of travel writing that included excerpts from Lund's diaries from Venezuela and the Antilles.

"I have it right here, over in that portfolio," he said, point-ing toward the counter. Berenice went into the shop and came back with the book.

On the way, her eyes had landed on the spine of the gray notebook, partially hidden under the receipts and invoices pil-ing up on the counter. The notebook was so much a part of her mother she didn't understand how it could be there while she wasn't.

"'We begin to grow weary,'" Mr. Müller read, "'of so much jungle, so much green, of so much grandiose, monotonous, and savage beauty. The truth is that we long for the ugliness of Man, the kind that reaches its most elevated expression on the old continent. What I would give for a bridge or even a mere fence to break up the landscape on occasion. I cannot but affirm that green is the most depressing of all colors. Two days ago, we climbed the eastern face of Mount Conception, in the direction of Topehya, where—I'd been assured—there lived a tribe known to the other natives as "those who came from the sea" and who had remained isolated from the rest of the country for centuries. When we finally arrive, I see a few huts barely standing around a muddy pond. There's smoke, some kind of chickens or wild turkeys running around, and bodies strewn across the dirt path. The first thing that comes to mind is that a fire or some natural catastrophe must have caught the residents by surprise; I think of Pompeii, but am immediately informed that this people always leaves a fire burning because they believe the sun will be extinguished one day and it is man's responsibility to illuminate the earth for all living creatures— this being the only way they, in their uselessness, can be of service. Keeping the flame and raising poultry are the only two occupations of this people, aside from collective divination. The Topehya do not have shamans. "They're all witches," my guide tells me in a whisper. I realize then that the residents—the elders, the adults, and the young—have collapsed wherever the end of the party caught them, and are now deep in a hallucinatory sleep. A man as wrinkled as a desert apricot has his arms wrapped around a gourd rattle. His family, two women and three children, lie beside him; they all have their left hand tucked into their armpit, and their forearms are bandaged in such a way that at first glance they appear to be missing. A few are, in fact, missing fingers or ears; others merely wear bandages over the latter. They are not all asleep: some have their eyes open and are smiling up at the sky, while others crawl around on their bellies. The smell of sweat, vomit, and excrement, of humans reduced to their bodily functions, is unbearable. As I approach one of the huts, I hear barking. Next to the opening that passes for a door I see a man sitting on his feet and digging a hole in the ground with his bare hands. He seems to be the only one awake. When I speak to him, however, he answers me with a growl and bares his teeth. My companions laugh and tell me I'm looking at a criollo who betrayed a rural leader from the area. His punishment was that they made him think he was a dog. Apparently the man has been like that for years. I understand in that moment how the people of Topehya have survived: by receiving clothes, animals, and other goods in exchange for their knowledge of albaria and other substances and, above all, for administering justice on behalf of their neighbors.'

"I should have warned your mother about this, about the power of suggestion in some hallucinogens," Mr. Müller said, closing the book. "But I skipped over that passage, too. It seemed too theatrical, an exaggeration that only showed Lund's fascination with the primitive. I focused on the pages where he describes the plant. Now that I've tried it, though, I can see it was a warning. Yes, I think so. I think the Dane knew very well what the consequences of consuming the plant were, which is why he described those scenes in such detail."

"I'm hungry," said Berenice, maybe because she didn't know what else to say, maybe because she was tired of keeping up the appearance of serenity and understanding for a world that didn't deserve it.

What Mr. Müller had just read to her sounded like a story, and she couldn't see the connection between the dog man and whatever had happened to her mother. But she did know one thing: it was about time someone let her act like a little girl.

9

Once she'd wrapped herself in the towel, the woman returned to the closet. Vik remained in the bathroom doorway, still playing his nebulous role of something between a guard and a butler. She reappeared a few seconds later, wearing another dress of coarse fabric, simple and white, just like the last one. A purse hung from her shoulder, though she didn't seem ready to go anywhere. She closed the closet door, leaned back against it, and stood there staring at him with drops falling from the tips of her hair, looking neither defeated nor defiant, more like someone who had just completed a mission and was waiting for a new one, or else had simply decided to dissolve into wet spots on the carpet.

Sitting at the kitchen table, she did nothing but eat (some bread and a few pieces of cheese). Vik tried the standard questions; he couldn't even get her to tell him her name. He had already passed through the different stages of anger (what most people called patience, Vik thought, was one of them, a kind of antechamber where rage collects before exploding). The friendly and vaguely ophidian tone that his father used at family gatherings had no effect, either. She responded by calmly crumbling a piece of bread, hunched over the table with her head nearly grazing its wooden surface, completely absorbed in the operation of pressing the crumbs into perfect little balls, which she lifted to her mouth one after another as he spoke. He abandoned the personal questions and tried with albaria, this time with a much more neutral tone, trying to avoid the word "addiction." He said things like "trip," "dream," and his favorites, the ones he'd heard throughout his childhood, "fake dawn" or "false light." He asked the woman how long she'd been using it and where she got it, since it was unlikely that the flower could grow naturally in that climate. Nothing. In the end, he pulled out a chair and sat in front of her. She hadn't stopped playing with her little balls of bread.

The story spilled from his lips without his meaning it to, filling the emptiness between them. Vik was surprised by how well he told it. It was the story of his first animal. But it was also the story of his brother, and Tania, and of life on the island of Coloma, in the city of Kent, where his parents had a mansion and their own train car for all the luggage they moved to their second house in the mountains on tracks the family had laid. His mother claimed it wasn't as hot there, that there weren't as many tourists, and that the polluted air of the capital was filtered by the garden's vines and ferns.

Life in Kent was divided into rain and sun, which for Vik meant hours either wasted at school, church, and the club, or won for excursions to the beach or the jungle. Prasad didn't mind the hours spent inside. He had more patience for adults. Vik, on the other hand, preferred useless collections and long walks on which he'd disappear for days with his maps marked with dead animals. In the end, those would determine his trajectory.

He also went with Prasad to his Ping-Pong matches. It was

one of the few things they did together. There was something about his brother's personality that came out in the sheltered environment of the club: a natural talent for social interaction and an ability to fill, with an anecdote or an anodyne joke, those awkward pauses in adult conversation that settled in between commentary on international events and complaints about the government, young people, or temporary workers. Prasad always provided the phrase the others needed in order to go on talking, the one that convinced them they were resolving major international issues from their tiny island. Vik could sense the contradiction even then.

The club was a stone building that had been part of the fortress and then the missions. Over the centuries, it had been a school, a convent, and a municipal building, until the British turned it into a gentlemen's club. But the spirit of the monks remained: in the symmetry of the arches and the extravagant wood, in the hallways of cool stone. Anyone could see that the terrace with a view of the sea, where the older members read the newspapers or watched badminton tournaments, was a recent addition that contradicted the buttonhole windows on the second floor. Vik liked to imagine the barbaric scenes those windows must have concealed. Not that he believed any of it. But he preferred any vestige of the old dominion to the measured style his father's family had brought to Coloma nearly a century ago, which replaced opinions with long-winded excuses.

The Spaniards hadn't thought much of the island. Columbus had passed it by on his second voyage, though he did note in his diary (in a passage all the children of Coloma learned by heart) the presence of "an island in the form of a bird, set apart from the others to the south of Redonda, which appears amply fertile, but upon which we did not disembark, finding the wind against us and given intervening small and middle-sized ones which appeared better." It would take them more than a century to reach the shore. When they did, it was only to hunt men who would die working the mills on the neighboring islands.

To Vik, the history of Santa María de la Coloma had the same perverse quality as the building that housed the club. Half volcanic rock and half tropical forest, before the conquest the island was called Koreli (smoke), so named by the indigenous peoples who came from other islands and eventually settled there. Of its original inhabitants (who were there long before and had no proclivity for building), there were no survivors. Nor did they baptize the landscapes—all that remained were a few tools used for fishing and navigation and paintings in the caves that opened onto the bay. There were many theories and legends about the tribe's disappearance, and all of them involved the flower.

It was said that the natives killed one another off in a hallucinatory war.

That they had eaten human flesh and angered their god, who had in turn upset the evolutionary balance of his followers.

That they'd lost the ability to speak.

That they'd let themselves die off as they lay on their backs in groups and stared into the false light, their blood slowing until it no longer reached their arms and legs, which were lost. That they'd become a tribe of enlightened cripples whom the inhabitants of other lands worshipped like gods, sending tribute on rafts and consulting them like oracles.

That they'd eventually lined up in a long procession and cast themselves into the volcano that gave the island its name. Or that they'd set off in their canoes to establish a nocturnal world on the continent, a world where they would never again be blinded by that hallucinated dawn.

When he was a boy, Vik had imagined them as dark, dismembered men and women, creatures who had decided to abandon their human form, as if to distinguish their race or species from the rest of the planet's inhabitants. In his mind, the Primevals were no more than those torsos propped up on trees or monstrosities composed half of flesh and half of wood—always enveloped in the smoke of the volcano or of albaria—that had become synonymous with horror and mutilation in the minds of Coloma's modern inhabitants. As a form of drug abuse prevention, mothers would tell these stories and others, in which merely touching the flower meant losing a finger or an entire hand. Two different colonial governments ordered incinerations to wipe it out; the albaria would come back strong with new strains, the worst of which—*Albaria syphilitica*—had soft blue or green veins on the underside of its petals.

At this point in the story, the woman in Vik's kitchen lifted her head and looked him in the eyes for the second time. She seemed to be enjoying herself. Outside, it had stopped snowing and noon was creeping up.

She lowered her eyes and stared at her hands.

"Your story doesn't frighten me, if that's what you're trying to do. Losing an appendage doesn't seem like such a high price to pay, considering what you get in exchange. I'd be willing to do without these two fingers, for example. I wouldn't even notice they were missing. I never really liked rings, and believe me, I never dreamt of a wedding band." She laughed, waving her left hand in front of Vik's eyes. Her teeth were very yellow. The laughter produced a fit of coughing.

"All I'm trying to do is understand why you've been in my house for so long."

"It hasn't been so long. Six days, exactly. I spent the ones before that training in the street. Choosing you and watching you. There's a nontransferrable kind of wisdom that comes from living without a roof over your head. Everyone should try it sometime. It's a real feat of disappearance. There were days when just the thought of separating myself from the wall, of sitting up and smoothing the wrinkles in the blanket wrapped around me up to my ears seemed more than I was capable of. That's how it is with the cold. It settles into you little by little during the night and you don't even notice. First it curls your toes, then your fingers, then your whole back, which gives in and suddenly you're inside a cocoon. Then the cold becomes a vacuum. Inside and out: nothing. Until moving is like forcing your body to transform. It takes incredible con-centration to wake each fiber, each muscle, each hair until— thanks only to its moldable resolve—that mass of aches and pains decides to have flesh again, limbs, orifices, a vagina. The surprise is that it chooses to be a woman every morning, and not something else."

Vik nodded, though he wasn't sure he understood what she was saying. Was she talking about a kind of meditation or an altered state of consciousness that could only be reached by subjecting the body to the most extreme circumstances? All his anger collected in his right fist, which he clenched hard. He was careful to keep it under the table. He looked at the young face in front of him. How many catastrophes had touched her life? A case of acne, maybe? Years of waiting for that boy she liked to notice she was alive? And yet, this person saw los-ing everything as a wonder. A revival of the worst Christian saints. At any other time, the comparison would have made him smile. But now he stifled that gesture, too, and limited himself to clenching his fist.

"A little more and it all would have been over," she went

on. "It was the condition for moving on to the next phase. Being as small and silent as the spiders that live with you in this house. We'd already done it in other houses, but not for as long. It's part of the program. Total invisibility. Most people never find us. When I started my training I spent two whole days in a woman's house. She was a manager at some multinational who spent all day away from home. I got bored: it wasn't enough of a challenge. But you had to go and ruin everything, didn't you? For the love of Christ or whatever god appears to you . . . who goes and puts cameras in their own house?"

Vik lowered his eyes, feeling the heat rise to his face, take it over. His body was betraying him, again. He was silently grateful that the color of his skin protected him from this added humiliation. It was true. He was ashamed to be taken for one of them, one of the Bobs or Toms who sacrificed all on the altar of private property.

Nearly whispering, he said: "No god appears to me."

He wasn't prepared for the intelligence of her retort, which cut him deeper than the insolence of her tone.

"Maybe that's your fucking problem. Maybe that's why you use a cane, get yourself prescriptions so you can drug yourself legally, and surround yourself with dead animals. Did you ever think of that?" She stuck two balls of bread in her mouth as she spoke. "You're just as crippled as your Indians. The trick is to be as enlightened."

She wasn't looking at him this time; she had her eyes fixed on *Rabbit with Watch*, which was partially visible through the arched doorway that connected the kitchen with the living room.

"You said you were going to tell me the story of your first animal." Her gaze abandoned the Ploucquet and ran across the clock on the wall. It wasn't noon yet. "Go on. We still have some time."

Why did he obey her? Why didn't he throw her out right that very moment? And what did she mean when she said they "still had some time"? Had she been studying him closely enough to know when his body gave out? It sounded like she was having trouble breathing, as if the air reached her already polluted with noise, but it didn't seem like she was under the effect of albaria. Vik wondered what his chances were of using his phone before she stopped him, or of stabbing her with one of the knives on the kitchen counter, but he knew all too well that he'd lost the advantage.

The memory of the strength and agility she'd brought into play a few hours earlier stifled those calculations and, along with them, the final reproaches of his conscience. He sighed, feeling the morphine take leave of his back. Anything to keep her talking, to not fall back into silence.

He went to the stove and put the kettle on, then reached into the cupboard and pulled out the wooden box where he kept his teas. He chose jasmine, counting each second of the interval. At least there were some things he could still choose. He clung to those choices, those advantages. To tea, of course. And also to words.

௸

Smithfield had his stroke two days after our third class. A few hours later, I sat down in front of this camera for the first time. Fact. Even though you don't know it. You told me to talk about whatever came to mind. When I stopped at your table and took a sip of that lavender-flavored tea you had there, I noticed that you were just as surprised as I was. But you pulled yourself together right away. You saw that distant look in my eyes, saw how it took the cup an eternity to reach my mouth, saw that I was walking as if my skeleton had turned in its letter of resignation and left this mass of limp flesh to fend for itself. You had the good taste not to ask questions. You pointed to the video-memory room and told me to talk. I started with the deer and the hunting club, when I really should have started with Frank and the things he said and did before he was visited by Dr. Alzheimer, when we were young and, no, we didn't want to change the world like you suggested once; what we wanted was to blow its thousand and one locks.

That Saturday was our first target practice. Frank had gotten the Lower Lake Club to lend us its shooting range, so that's where we headed at lunchtime, to make the most of it before the real marksmen arrived (the club's steering committee adheres to the county's tacit rule of "no drinking, shooting, or gambling before two p.m.").

Before that, each student had to get their own gun. Except for Tom and Betty Paz—who discovered two old Winchesters in the basement of their home, saved by some miracle from their last garage sale—everyone had to pick their own. Most of them ignored my advice about range and caliber. Elizabeth showed up with one of those modern rifles with the telescopic sights and a dozen accessories she bought online. Maggie and Heather solved the problem by opening a bank account—along with your debit card, they give you a Weatherby Mark V, an expensive rifle with a royal pedigree, but it gets the job done. The only one who really picked his gun was Max Cercone. His eldest son went with him to the neighborhood armory. After holding several rifles to his shoulder to test their weight and the feel of the stock, he picked a Henry, one of the least popular guns on the market because it's heavy and only works at close range.

I brought my old Marlin. I could almost hear it singing in my hands after all those years of boredom on the rack above my fireplace. Unfortunately, the old Marlin remembers the last time it saw action more clearly than I do. Going back to the woods is a way of forgetting that day, of sanitizing it. No hunting rifle wants to retire after blowing a young woman's brains out.

It was Max who surprised me most. He couldn't sign a check if you handed him a pen. And forget about using scissors or carrying a cup of coffee from the kitchen to the table. It's always a catastrophe. But things change when you put something heavy in his hands. He was the first one to find his stance with the rifle. Contrary to what most people think, there isn't just one way to hold the barrel or one place to rest the stock. Max found his quickly. It's not elegant, but it works. As far as his aim goes, with practice and a little persistence, he could probably do all right with a stationary target. But I doubt he'll ever be good enough to hit anything in motion.

Anyone who's watched Mr. and Mrs. Paz shoot can see they're rediscovering the couple they were a long time ago. The activity has rejuvenated them; now I understand why they were the first ones to sign up for my class. Tom never walks as tall or carries himself with as much composure as when he leans ceremoniously over his Winchester. Betty's a pretty decent shot, but she gets tired quickly. Fifteen minutes of practice and she's already sitting on her cloth folding chair (she never leaves home without it) and shooting from there, with predictably unfortunate results.

When Elizabeth shoots, her whole body goes tense and she holds her breath. Exactly the opposite of what I've been telling them. All she accomplishes with that is to knock herself even further off balance when the rifle kicks. I've explained it to her dozens of times, but she seems incapable of following instructions. She nods without ever taking her eyes off the target, her finger still on the trigger. I think Ron's death did away with the last of her neurons. I haven't seen anyone in that condition since the Bridgend days.

Maggie and Heather Armstrong are the complete opposite. They hang off every word when I explain something, but when it's time to put it into practice, I always catch them fighting between themselves. Maggie is in charge of taking notes in a black notebook. She's very conscientious. I imagine she was a perfect mother and wife (she has two daughters who visit her twice a month without fail), but that won't get her far in the woods. Behind all that consideration there's an insecure creature dying for attention, terrible characteristics for a hunter. Nothing like Heather, who's curt when she's not being outright rude. All it takes is one look at her with the rifle in position to see she's got potential: she stands with her feet at forty-five degrees and leans forward until her cheek grazes the stock of her Weatherby. Then she shoots. Her aim is pretty bad, but it doesn't matter. Fact. There are some things you can't learn through practice, they're just in your genes. And Heather's a natural shot.

Emilia was still with us that day. As far as I remember, she only stayed for a few minutes and just watched the shooters, making comments and offering encouragement. She said that her rehabilitation prohibited her from carrying a gun, that her contribution was going to be purely "logistical." Can you imagine.

Frank and I kept an eye on the six students from a prudent distance, behind the glass at their backs. I went in and out: demonstrating, correcting, suggesting. He was unusually talkative, even though he never took his eyes off them as he spoke, as if he was still trying to convince himself he was in a shooting range. The more I think about it, the harder it is for me to reproduce exactly what we said that day. It wasn't easy to keep a conversation going with all those interruptions. I remember he was interested in technique. He said that he was thinking of getting a gun and taking the class himself. I told him it wasn't a good idea, that he needed to stay in the shadows. A group always needs a voice in the shadows. At Bridgend it had been Clarke and Gutierrez. Now it was his turn, I said.

He looked away from Elizabeth, who at that moment was celebrating her first decent shot with Max, and said:

"This has nothing to do with Bridgend, Berilia."

He tried to keep his tone light, but it still crushed the small feeling of triumph I had that day.

"Of course not," I offered, trying to stay afloat.

"This isn't about the past. This is about the future."

(Like it or not, he was already a voice in the shadows, and a pretty corny one, at that. I decided not to point this out.)

"I'm not doing this for the future. I'm doing this for us."

I felt the heat rush across my face.

"Of course," he said. Then came what I was most afraid of. "But also for those who come after us. One must leave a legacy. Gabi thinks so, too. I went to see her a little while ago. It was cold, even though the sun was out. You know how she believes in community more than any of us. But she's wrong, even if it had been a sunny day and she were surrounded by flowers (you should see what she's done with a few of them, incredible grafts and the most spectacular colors). You can't be democratic with these things. No, I tell her, even good things turn into poison when they're not taken in moderation. And there are punishments. No one leaves the scene without paying their bill. And you pay it in this world, not any other. Are you sure the Marlin wasn't under your bed? Johnny says they looked for it everywhere. Seems there's too many pigeons around his building."

I had no idea who this Johnny was. But I tightened my grip on the rifle before responding. I'd answered that question a thousand times.

That day, the one Smithfield seemed trapped in, I couldn't find my left shoe and had crouched down to look for it under what had been my bed for the past few weeks. I already said that Gabi, Celeste, and I were sleeping in the same room. Seemed like the best thing for the baby. But it's also true that the mattresses on the floor had begun to annoy me, just like the cockroaches that climbed over me at night and just like other people's sweat. All sure signs that I was already on my way back. No, the Marlin wasn't where I'd left it.

"She must have taken it with her early, Frank, when she left the house."

"Of course, of course. How stupid of me. She was going after the deer, right? The one she always talked to at dawn. What was its name? She'd have long conversations with it and always come back upset. Not advisable. Deep down, I think she was already anticipating this," he said, gesturing vaguely to the firing lanes. "What we had to do."

"That's right," I lied.

No, Gabi wasn't going after the deer. She was going after herself. She'd gotten lost somewhere in the Big Party, and there was no substance or song or lover that could bring her back anymore.

Same as Smithfield. Dr. Alzheimer had clearly paid him a visit, or maybe something much worse. If I'd had any doubts about it, they vanished that day at the shooting range. But I decided to go on, anyway. Not for the six students sweating in the racket of their inexperience. Not because I believed that the deer had gone crazy, or that they were a hazard to the environment or to humanity. Not even for Frank or for an "us" that (oh, I knew all too well) didn't exist. For me. Of course. It's for me that I went on, that I go on.

∞

As he served her liverwurst-and-cucumber sandwiches, Mr. Müller told her everything he knew. Or everything he thought he knew, since Berenice was not inclined to accept without proof any story that confirmed her abandonment. According to him, Emma's conversion had begun in the final weeks of summer, when she'd started providing albaria to the people living in the woods and (he was even more sure of it now) consuming it herself from time to time.

August was coming to an end when two customers—a woman with long thick blond hair and a tall man with a broad back and a foreign look to him—caught the former pharmacist's attention: they always showed up as the sun was going down and always used the back door. Emma would go out, hand them a kraft paper envelope, and they would disappear into the trees. He could tell they were dropouts by how they'd aged prematurely. They were barefoot and their clothes were shabby: she wore a dirty dress over a pair of jeans, and he was in gray pants with hems eaten away by life at the mercy of the elements, and a button-down shirt that had once been black but was now an indeterminate milky color. He looked like an executive who'd lost his mind in the middle of a board meeting and had been adopted late in life by wolves. He was very blond, his beard and hair were long, and he spoke with an accent. Mr. Müller had confirmed this a few days ago, when he'd gotten close enough to listen in on the conversation they were having with Emma. Several days earlier, he'd taken the precaution of stealing a couple of leaves from the albaria while Emma was arguing with a couple about the price of centerpieces for their wedding. Mr. Müller didn't know what he'd use them for, but he was certain they'd come in handy at some point, even if only to prove that the plant was real. But was it? If he'd learned anything about albaria, it's that it was all too easy to confuse it with similar strains, or even with run-of-the-mill salvia.

"Yesterday, at exactly seven thirty in the evening, I confirmed that it was the *lundiana* strain," he said, biting into his fourth sandwich and looking at Berenice's watch. "I finally had the nerve to chew a fistful of leaves, and then I fell asleep. I thought it would be better to do it here, so I could still keep an eye on the flower shop. They weren't even fresh leaves; they'd been in my freezer for a while. I can only say one thing: there's a reason Lund's tribe called it sweet dream. At first, I didn't feel anything, maybe just a slight dizziness that made me sit down on the cot. I must have stayed like that for hours, staring at a stain on the wall. I entered a lethargic state during which I was suddenly struck by an expansive ray of white light. No, it wasn't a ray, because a ray is finite. This was bigger and more overwhelming. Like a wave or a sun. Yes, a white sun flooded my mind and I stopped being me, I mean, I stopped being this person with desires, worries, and ideas, and was simply part of the wave of light in my head, which slowly settled into a fascination with the things around me, especially the ant that was and was not me and which I'd never be able to touch, no matter how much I stretched my arm, but which I could perceive in all its perfection, I could see, no, each of those six legs was a part of me and I could feel them scratching their way along the supple plaster of the wall, I could be inside that insistence, be one with that impulse for work and resignation.

Then the happiness, that clumsy ignorance, disappeared. The light released me and I fell back into this consciousness, into this reasoned cancer we call life."

Berenice would have liked to understand what Mr. Müller meant by "clumsy ignorance." The only image those words called to mind was Baby Moon trying to keep her balance in the circle of dolls who excluded her. But Baby Moon's clumsiness was a problem; there wasn't anything easy or happy about it. Mr. Müller was mixing things up. *Because he does drugs*, said a voice in her head that sounded like Emma Lynn, but that couldn't have been her because Emma Lynn would never say that. She thought everyone had a right to go crazy. So it was possible she'd sold hallucinogenic leaves to the people from the woods. She could even imagine her doing it with pride and good business sense.

Berenice sighed, took a sip of the beer that Mr. Müller had served her with a slice of orange in it, and asked him to tell her what happened the last time the two dropouts came to the flower shop.

That afternoon, last Monday, he'd gone over to the fence he'd erected to separate his house from what had been his garage and was now his renter's shop. Mr. Müller liked to keep commercial matters clear and separate. From his living room window, he'd seen the man and woman arrive. He closed the curtains and went out to the garden, pretending he was looking for Sissy, the dog, who was sleeping comfortably in front of his television at that moment. Sometimes, if it wasn't too cold, he'd let her loose so she could get some exercise (like her master, Sissy had a weight problem). He got close enough to realize that the three of them were arguing: Emma, with her back against the nursery doorway; the others, too close to her and leaning in. He couldn't really make out what they were saying, but it was clear that Emma had decided not to give any more albaria leaves to the group, which made perfect sense, Mr. Müller concluded, because otherwise she was going to kill the only plant she had. Apparently they didn't reach an agreement, because the man and woman refused to leave and went on talking for a long time. They were trying to convince Emma to go back to the woods with them. The man said they wanted to show her something "incredible." The woman took a few steps back so he was closer to Emma. Mr. Müller had felt he should intervene. He called for Sissy again, and the woman shifted nervously. Emma didn't even hear him. That was when he noticed something that had escaped his observational skill the other times: Emma was staring into the giant Scandinavian's eyes as if she'd sunk all the way down in them.

"She was obviously in love with him. Now, I ask you: How is it possible women keep falling into that trap? So many brassieres burned in feminist bonfires, and they all end up accepting the same fate. Your mother seemed different, but, well. That was when I realized she hadn't even been selling them the plant: she'd been giving it to them, first the leaves, and then the few seeds she must have had left. She'd been collaborating with them, with their project, somehow. Sure. She'd given in to his words, his ideas, or—even worse—to his pheromones. The guy took a step toward her, reached out, and ran his thumb down her cheek. That was enough. Emma went into the nursery and came back out with a leather bag she slung over her red coat. That, and the pot with the albaria, was all I saw her take. They'd convinced her that they'd solved the mystery of how it grows."

Not true, thought Berenice. The flower didn't matter. Neither did the man. What mattered, she realized at the exact moment Mr. Müller paused to finish another beer, was Gabi.

Berenice went to the counter and came back with the gray notebook. She found the photograph of the men and women lined up in front of the house that looked like a castle, waved it in front of Mr. Müller's eyes, and told him about the day she and her mother had found the seeds hidden in the lining of her backpack. She told him that, and also everything Emma had said about Gabi and her life in that home of turrets and balconies. Berenice couldn't believe her mother had lived there, even if it was only for the first few months of her life. Seven or nine. No one knew for sure. Months during which those men and women had taken turns feeding her, changing her diapers, calming her when she cried. Until Grandma Cecilia arrived to rescue her from "that abomination."

Gabi wasn't in the photo because it had been taken a little while before she'd arrived at the mansion. Cecilia used to tell Emma how her daughter had run off in the middle of the night with her backpack, a guitar, and the firm conviction that she had outwitted the whole family. The next morning, Cecilia and her other children had relived, between bites of pancakes and bouts of laughter, how each of them had held their breath and pretended to be fast asleep, shaking in their sheets at the thought that the eldest might change her mind, that when all was said and done she wouldn't have the courage to abandon them.

Gabi wanted to be a singer, to record albums and play shows in venues packed with young people. But she was lazy, she lacked discipline. All she had was a voice. Cecilia had always thought that Gabi didn't deserve it, that she squandered it with every word that left her mouth. The fact that such a voice belonged to her daughter made her question the universe's distribution of gifts.

Several months before her daughter ran away, Cecilia discovered that Gabi had stopped going to the piano classes she'd been paying for. She let her be, and waited. She let her stuff the money for Miss Dalessio into a can. She let her save up for her bus ticket, let her plan, hoping that eventually she'd get lost. Exactly the way she did. In that house of the rich and insane.

When Emma told Berenice the story of her mother, on the other hand, she never talked about perdition or gifts, or the accounting on which the universe rested. She told it like a legend that explained her birth: Gabi's adventures in the Bridgend commune were about a poor girl spending time in a palace where music and psychedelia turned every man into a would-be rock-and-roll idol and free love was part of a contract signed with the legend, the natural response to so much talent. Grandma Cecilia had raised Emma Lynn and taught her everything she knew, but she'd also made her the same as everyone else (the same as her aunts and uncles, who did their hair in styles that had been out of fashion for fifteen years, who went to church, who bought houses with backyards, and who had at least three children each). Gabi was her mystery, her restlessness and her beauty, the shadow of the woman she could be and who lay in wait in her genes, tormenting her, waiting for the right moment to pounce. Berenice didn't know any of this. But she sensed it. She sensed that her mother hadn't abandoned her, she'd simply decided to head for that fairy tale where she, Celeste Emma Lynn Brown, suddenly and before it all ended, had been born.

10

His first animal had been a bird, a run-of-the-mill canary. It had belonged to Tania, the girl he and Prasad had fought over without admitting it, or maybe without even knowing it, for a few years when they were young. She lived in an enormous sky-blue house made of wood on the corner of Kent's main avenue and the street where the church was. The Cardelús family was poor: she cleaned houses; he drank and, when necessary, led a small-scale smuggling ring that moved things on and off the island. In those days, the family would pass through spasms of prosperity that vanished along with the cases of whiskey that arrived from the mainland. Tania had gotten used to this pattern. Instead of dreaming about dresses, makeup, or music albums, she collected birds. The veranda of the house was full of cages.

The canary wasn't even her favorite; vying for that honor were a black-naped oriole her father had gotten her and an old macaw she'd bought for loose change at a fair. It could say "whore" in Spanish, English, and French. Vik found the birds fairly repellent. As a young boy, he'd developed an exaggerated sensitivity to odors (he hated anything fried, aged cheeses, his mother's perfumes). This refined sense of smell would keep him from the true heights of the taxidermist's passion. He preferred the later stages of the work: stuffing and mounting, repairs and maintenance.

Tania didn't bother to clean the cages, so they were always full of excrement and food scraps. And then there was the noise, as if the birds were competing for the attention of their mistress who, lying in the faded hammock that hung across from their cages or playing Scrabble on the floor of the veranda with Vik and his brother, would goad them on with calls and whistles in a maddening conversation. Vik always found it much more interesting to identify differences in their plumage, coloring, and anatomy than to concentrate on the absurd and even grotesque song of each species.

This fascination with form had led him to study death. He marked down in a notebook how many days it took the body of a stray cat, poisoned by someone in the neighborhood, to decompose; he carried maps marked with crosses where a hatchling had fallen from its nest or an iguana had been squashed. He would return to those places just to observe the process that followed. He was particularly intrigued by nature's ability to dispose of the bodies, which disappeared long before they had fully decomposed. As if some deity of the jungle took them away during the night so as not to disrupt the spectacle of life.

It was on one of those excursions, on the way from their house in the mountains to the club, that he and Prasad discovered a patch of albaria. Prasad never participated in his explorations and had only agreed to stray from the path because there was still time before the more important members arrived at the club. At fifteen, he had already developed the ability to read that other kind of map, of groups and their hierarchies, something that would prove to be worth much more in his corporate career than his bachelor's degree in psychology and the master's in business he got abroad.

In a closed-off area thick with vegetation, amid a cluster of rocks that still held water from the last rains, albaria was growing. The brothers had only ever seen the Flower of Consciousness in books and paintings. Without daring to touch the white-petaled specimens, they argued about whether this was albaria or a similar plant. They didn't remember reading anywhere that it was so small. Vik had imagined it the size of a lotus, or at least a lily, but it wasn't even as big as a daisy. With a twig, Prasad confirmed the presence of grayish lines on the underside of the flowers. Vik still wasn't convinced. That was when his brother thought of the only way to prove it beyond the shadow of a doubt. Covering his hand with a plastic bag (a completely unnecessary precaution that only revealed the power that the national myth held over their young minds), he cut off four flowers and a few leaves; then, without revealing a single detail of his plan, he gave them to Vik to keep in his backpack.

That afternoon they went to Tania's house after leaving the club. While she tried to make them something to drink out of two wrinkled limes, Vik watched Prasad put juice from the plant (which he'd previously mashed inside the plastic bag) into the canary's water. The afternoon went by like any other. The same sounds and smells. The same board games. As the sun went down and the time came to say goodbye, Tania noticed that the bird wasn't moving. Prasad changed the subject with a joke about the island's cricket team and the brothers left the house without getting caught.

The next day, Vik went to visit Tania earlier and alone. He found her in the hammock, her face soiled with tears. When she saw him, she just pointed at the canary's cage. The bird was lying on its side, rigid.

"He spent the entire night slamming himself against the bars. Over and over again, like he wanted to hurt himself. Until he did."

Vik approached the cage. There was no trace of blood. The hemorrhage must have been internal.

Tania had two other canaries. Vik sat beside her and tried, in vain, to comfort her by citing this figure. She hung from his neck. Vik didn't know what to do with his arms (he would always be too young for this barefoot, disheveled, beautiful girl). The idea came to him like the solution to an equation or the logical conclusion of a story. He stood and grabbed the cage with the canary.

"Don't worry, there's a solution," he said, and left the house as Tania shouted something unintelligible at him from the veranda.

Vik had read about the process in encyclopedias and non-fiction books. When he reached his parents' summer home, he went around back to the gardener's shed, which had sat abandoned for years. After gathering his instruments, he made an incision in the canary's belly and began emptying the cavity with a crochet hook, allowing the blood to drain into the sink. He was amazed there was so little of it, and that it didn't smell like anything in particular. Then he set about severing joints, starting with the bird's legs and then moving on to where its wings met its body. The hardest part was doing this without damaging or dirtying its feathers, especially because his mother's knives and scissors were sharp, but were too big for the task. He worked all day and night, manipulating the bird's ghost until it was an unrecognizable entity, a red-and-yellow veneer laid onto a board. He tied a string to the animal's skull and, using pieces of wood in different sizes, reconstructed its form, over which he stretched the skin he'd previously sprayed with camphor. Then he filled the whole thing with straw and cotton and closed the incision with the most delicate stitches his ten years allowed him. Its eyes were two black pearls from a broken necklace he found in his mother's sewing basket. When he'd inserted them, he took two steps back and gasped.

The bird was a bird again.

Vik didn't remember feeling especially powerful, or thinking—like Akerman or Hornaday—that death is not an end but merely an accident. He'd thought only of Tania, of the moment he would give her back her canary. Yes, he'd imagined the scene with the satisfaction of someone who believes they possess the secret to another's happiness.

"Come to think of it," he reflected in his kitchen, face to face with the woman who'd been hiding in his closet, "that secret is the only thing that gives you any real power. Even if it doesn't last," he concluded, serving their tea in two pink-and-gold porcelain cups.

"To hold someone else's happiness in your hands . . . what a burden. And what a power trip, too," she replied.

Vik thought to himself that he agreed with her, but didn't say anything. He smiled, pleased by how she'd willingly entered into conversation, and sped to the end of the story. Confiding secrets, especially unhappy ones, always worked on women.

The next morning, the boy who would soon call himself Vik (and not Brian Vikram, as his parents had baptized him) stuck the canary in its cage, draped a cloth over the top, and walked to Tania's house. He didn't find her on the veranda. He heard her voice upstairs; she must have been in her father's study. They weren't fighting, only talking, but everyone in that house shouted when they spoke, probably because of the birds. Vik uncovered the cage, placed it in the corner where it had been, and lay down in the hammock to wait for Tania.

He was awakened by her screams, followed by her father's laughter. Mr. Cardelús rarely came down to the living room or the veranda, but there he was, enveloped in the smoke of a cigar as thick as the lips that held it, the buttons of his shirt straining across his stomach. He was holding the canary's cage at eye level and saying, half in English and half in Spanish or French, "Monstrous, truly monstrous," as he laughed, leaving a trail of cigar ashes to mark his course around the veranda.

"My daughter and I have been discussing the death of this bird." Mr. Cardelús brought the cage to his nose and then leaned over Vik. "A poison that drives its victim mad and leaves no trace, it would seem."

Tania remained in the doorway. She stared with horror at the mute, inflated creature that had once been her canary.

It wasn't hard for them to extract a confession from Vik. They were less interested in his and Prasad's motives than in the exact location of the albaria. Tania's father had been trying to find the Flower of Consciousness for years.

A few months later, Vik got a job as a taxidermist's apprentice at the Museum of Coloma. Mrs. Cardelús ran off to Europe with one of her employers, and Tania and her father started the first commercial market in the region for albaria. Young people began to arrive from all over. They looked like they'd been mass-produced in a factory on the continent, with their long hair and skin as translucent and pink as a lizard's. They spent hours splayed out on the beach, preaching free love to the local girls. They all had a crust of dirt around their necks, which they wore like a countercultural badge of honor. All of them, in one way or another, were searching for or ended up finding the flower.

Vik never returned to the Cardelús home and never got the chance to console Tania for the many other losses she would suffer in her life.

The canary was thrown out with the rubbish that same day.

Prasad kept winning Ping-Pong tournaments, oblivious to these catastrophes and all the others that would visit the island.

༄

Because the Marlin isn't the only one that needs to forget. I need to head out to the woods, too. I need a deer I can track night and day like my life depends on it, too. Fact. Some people reach the end having eaten in the best restaurants, danced in the fanciest ballrooms, and participated in everything that excites and astonishes the masses, but without ever having felt the pleasure of individuality, the power of the unmistakable self. Contrary to popular belief, introspection is not the world's most common activity. In fact, most people avoid that encounter. Our entire social system is designed for us to avoid it. That's why in that final moment, most people look around and are certain they've forgotten something. Hard to put into words. I'd say it's life itself, wearing a tattered party dress and with the puffy eyes of an old jazz singer, staring up at them from the filthy gutter they've tossed it into. Fact. Some people scrap their lives too early, without even realizing it. That's how most of them go, still worried about their mortgage payment or the phlegm in their lungs, both knowing and hiding that knowledge until the very last moment, without the courage or the strength to make any demands.

I forget it myself, sometimes. Like I said, it's hard to resist

so many opportunities for confusion. That Saturday, for example, I could have really talked with Frank, I could've made an
effort to wring out of him the man he used to be, the man he
could still be. But I didn't. I focused on the task at hand (how
much better is it to have something practical to do; if you think
I'm kidding, just look at all the marriages that have been saved
by the silver that needs polishing every month, the clothes
that should be aired out every summer, the gardens in need of
pruning, the saints demanding worship). I focused, then, on
the task of turning those six old folks into a group with a skill.
With a skill and a purpose.

I'm perfectly aware of my selfishness. I know. I'm a deeply
selfish woman. But that's not the worst possible sin. Honest
selfishness is preferable to by-the-book generosity. And yeah,
I wanted him to look at me with love in his eyes when he said
goodbye. And yeah, I chose seeing what I wanted to see over
seeing his indifference. Anyone want to blame me for that? No?
Didn't think so.

At nine thirty in the morning the Tuesday after our target practice, as he was giving his assistant instructions about
changing the dioramas in the Hall of Man, Smithfield had his
"cerebrovascular accident." Fact: even blood gets tired of making the same rounds all the time. I didn't see him; I was helping
with two school visits, and arrived after the ambulance had
taken him away. I had to hear about it from his assistant, who
alternated tears and irrelevant details (he insisted on telling me
how Smithfield had smiled involuntarily while giving his direc-
tives, as if the corners of his mouth were being pulled upward)
with an awareness of how superfluous he was to the story. I
let him talk. Someone asked me if I wanted to go to the hospital. I said no. I came here instead. I hadn't planned to. I left
the museum at noon and just started walking. Chance decided

that you were going to arrive early and that there wasn't going to be anyone else at the center. You and your lavender tea. You and your fantasy that seniors matter.

There you have it. So far we've had one tracking class without him, and the group didn't seem too upset by his absence. Like I said, they don't care. The next Saturday we did more practice, but this time in the woods. There's a place on Amarillo Hill, not too far from Elizabeth Jackson Duda's house (she only took her husband's name after he died) that's great for drills. Miles of undeveloped woodland—nothing but trees, gullies, and streams—stretching all the way to Concordia Cemetery, the oldest one in the city. Most foreigners like you don't know it, but there are bodies buried there from the colonial period. It's also a favorite spot for the deer. In fact, that's where they enter the city from. So it's doubly useful for us, as a practice range and also as a final objective. I'm sure Ron Duda's buck beds down somewhere in those woods. When all is said and done, though, none of this matters. Like I said. We don't care. In these uncertain times, I'm sure of just one thing: this is the moment to make demands, to give that old lady in the tattered dress a good shake and push her back out onto the stage. From now on, no more distractions. From now on, it's just Beryl Hope and one objective: to recognize and register each of the thousand and one ways I'm alone in the world. Just like my uncle Ben. There's a real pleasure in that knowledge, in finally solving the mystery. In knowing it's me—me minus the world, me, Beryl Hope—I'm the animal in flight.

cr̃e

"Perhaps," Mr. Müller acknowledged as he set aside the photograph in which he'd just recognized a classmate from college, "what these people are looking for is the continuation of a dream. Your mother, too. Why not? I don't know. I remember ideas like these were all over the magazines when I was young. I couldn't even tell you, really, what it was all about. In those days I was married and had two children to support. Rebellion is for the rich, it always has been. And it still is. I promise you, those lunatics preaching a return to nature, dereliction of civic duties, and a life of delirium out in the woods never knew hardship. They're a bunch of overfed kids. Sure. They've binged on technology, speed, and information, and now they've decided to purge for a while by going back to Thoreau, or Ginsberg, or someone new. Their challenges to the status quo are just vacation dissidence. To someone who has everything, having nothing must seem like heaven. I confirmed it that day in the woods: there's nothing but words there. Sure. Smoke and mirrors.

"Now, anyone else in my position would have gone home, back to the peace and quiet of their couch and the company of their pet. But I decided to follow them. I guess you could say I was worried about your mother. I wanted at least to be sure she was acting of her own free will and wasn't under the influence of any plant. Okay, I also wanted to know what those people were really doing out there in the woods. It's always perplexed me that curiosity has such a bad reputation in our culture. It killed the cat and is behind all of humanity's ills? Please. I'm sure that in some part of the world far wiser and more civilized than our own, curiosity is revered as a deity with eyes as big as dinner plates. Without curiosity, there are no scientific advances. Without curiosity, there would be no novels or movies, no future. So I decided to follow them. As long as there was light, at least.

"I let them get pretty far ahead, to avoid suspicion. Your mother's coat was easy to see from a distance, and besides, I know the woods at least as well as they do. I thought they'd go farther in, that they'd have a secret hiding place, but no. I think that's part of their success: they move around all the time and are broken up into different groups; they're not one single community. The state of things these days works in their favor, too: there are so many abandoned houses, farms, hospitals, and schools in the countryside that it's easy for them to find shelter and move every so often from place to place. Sure. I imagine they also have a system of degrees and hierarchies; there are cults that work like that, that keep some members in the dark and conceal even the names of their leaders. The point is, the four of us walked for less than an hour, with them in front, and me following behind, relaxed because I'd figured out right away they were headed for the abandoned hotel. You've probably heard of it. It's in the valley. It used to be a spot for newlyweds. Built by a Romanian immigrant in the late forties. Seems he had a monumental and monotonous idea of love and what happens on your wedding night, because the place has two hundred enormous rooms, all decorated in pink and white, with thick curtains and carpeting, and each with a heart-shaped bathtub. I think at one point there was even an ice rink and a swimming pool with the same design. Only the tennis court escaped the theme.

When I was young, business was already in decline. Andreescu overestimated the power of the unions and the railroad. No one takes trains anymore; the tracks are abandoned and there aren't any more workers dreaming of romance in the mountains. These days, there are trees growing by the reception desk, the tiles are covered in mildew, and someone has found it amusing to gather the television sets from all the rooms and stack them against the wall of the ballroom in an arrangement meant to look like a giant electronic heart. I imagine the dropouts are responsible for that bit of irony, too. A sad heart, beating to the rhythm of its cathode tubes. Or it would be, if the place still had electricity. It doesn't. Or gas, or any other kind of energy, except what that bunch of crazies has managed to bring to it.

"They hold their meetings in the ballroom. What used to be a fountain in the middle of it, a Venus being born out of some rocks, was now a bonfire; it seemed to have been burning for a long time, because the statue was all black, so I figure the hotel has served as a meeting place for a while.

"In a building like that, it was easy to find a place to hide. It was already dark by the time I got there, so all I had to do was stand behind a velveteen curtain by one of the broken windows. Your mother, the man, and the blonde were with another ten or twelve people gathered in a circle around a bonfire. The only light in that enormous room was coming from the fire, which left the corners in absolute darkness. My eyes were slow to adjust, so it took me a while to notice certain key details, like the corral and the fact that, just as in Lund's account, some of the participants wore bandages on their fingers or ears.

"'Here we are,' said the foreigner, gesturing toward Emma, 'with a new force come to join itself to ours. Brothers and sisters, there is a time for war and a time for peace. The time for peace is long over. War has long been upon us—a global, ecological, and religious conflict that our governments choose to ignore. The war between Death and Life. We're all aware that the path of political or economic solutions is too comfortable, too reassuring, too self-indulgent. Brothers and sisters, this is a battle for survival. Ask Teo and Angela, who stand here among us: they've survived the most outrageous atrocities and have decided to declare themselves son and daughter. Offspring.

Child. Just think of the words—their happiness, their innocence. Ask the animals here among us . . .' At this point, the
foreigner gestured toward the corral, where three young deer
were observing the scene. 'They know it better than any of us;
ask the fervent ecologists who don't yet dare to join our ranks.
They know it, too. World War Three began decades ago and
it's being waged silently but effectively by men with short hair
and custom technology, whose only objective is to destroy the
mysterious lattice of life, the strings that bind us impercepti-
bly but indisputably to the planet. I know because I used to be
one of them. Another cog. Until I woke up. Until I decided to
deprogram myself, drop out, go invisible. Like each one of
you. In the face of that genocidal corporate machine, there's
no other option. Neutrality isn't possible. You're either part of
the death apparatus, or you choose life. This one, the only one
we have. In this struggle, the only valid strategy is the one that
runs through our veins, the one all organic life employs for survival: resist. And what does that mean? There are seven kinds
of resistance. We need to resist lovingly, supporting all the sisters and brothers who choose to live in hiding. But also to resist
passively: refusing to collaborate, abandoning, renouncing.
There are sisters and brothers who choose active resistance
every day: sabotaging and blocking corporate and government
communication networks, hacking their computers, making
their planes disappear, destroying every last one of the death
machines they've put on the earth. Welcome. There are also
ways to resist publicly: declaring life and denouncing death.
But we need, above all, to resist biologically: be healthy and
conspire in sex and love, but not in the seed and the rearing,
which only bring new problems to a world that hasn't been
sustainable for a while. Maybe one day we'll deserve reproduction. But for now, we've lost that right. Which is why we

need, also and above all, to resist spiritually: awaken the true life in you any way you can—through pain, through cold or hunger, and sometimes, only sometimes, through the natural substances here for that purpose, which we should use with wisdom. Resist as the animals do. Go out and be witnesses like them. And, finally, resist symbolically: go find in that world the Big Sibling who will guide you toward the innocence we lost with the invention of the prison we call language. We have not yet managed to free ourselves from that cage.' Here the man paused, looked around the room, and added, 'But we will.'

"'We will,' they all repeated. And the next thing I saw, the foreigner picked a few leaves from your mother's albaria and started dividing them among those present. She took some, too. And she did it without ever taking her eyes off the man. She was really intoxicated by him. I imagine she must still be; if not, she'd be back."

Berenice did everything she could to follow Mr. Müller's story, but only a few meaningless images came to mind, along with a deep, heavy drowsiness that made it hard for her to concentrate, and that contained enormous stone hearts with people doing obscene things in them; deer banging their heads against the bars of their cages, trying to break free; her mother and the man with the long blond hair on the back of a motorcycle, going full speed down an asphalt road. Berenice understood this last part most clearly because it went with the word "intoxicated," which Mr. Müller had used more than once. She could see clearly how Emma had finally become Celeste thanks to that word, how she wrapped her arms around the man's waist with a triumphant glint in her eyes, which had turned blue from so much joy. Berenice could even see the clothes her mother was wearing: jeans, leather boots, a colorful blouse, and a scarf tied around her hair. She had a guitar slung over her shoulder. Yes, it was easy to picture Emma Lynn running away from her, from Great-grandma Cecilia, and from the flowers, by way of intoxication. She understood. Now all she wanted was for Mr. Müller to be quiet and let her forget about it all.

But he kept talking for a while longer, taking his time to explain his thinking. He'd reached the part of the story that interested him most, and someone needed to hear it. He didn't care if Berenice understood half of what he said, or if she fell asleep with her elbows propped on the nursery table. Someone needed to know that he, Alfred Müller, on his way home and building on pure conjecture, had solved the mystery of albaria.

In a way he didn't understand completely, it occurred to Vik—who was unsettled or exhausted the way someone who has just told too long a story can be—that he was responsible for the woman looking at him across his kitchen table. He and his childhood discovery.

"You said it was the story of your first animal. I thought you were talking about something else. About the plant, its effects. Not that," she said, slamming her hand down on the table. She didn't do it particularly hard, but the contact was loud enough to startle Vik. "So this means you never tried it," she went on, disappointed.

"Of course I never tried it. It was enough for me to see what it did to that bird. Or do you think animal suicide is a normal occurrence?"

"Fine. We've seen a couple animals go crazy out in the woods. They run around frantic for hours. But that's all. Nothing like what you're describing. Nothing's ever happened to our deer, but maybe that's because they only eat the seeds. Ever since that six-point buck got away, Aero's been really careful about that."

"You can't apply the term 'crazy' to that world. We don't have words for it, for a bird that goes against its every natural instinct and slams itself like that against the bars of its cage."

"It takes courage, that's true."

She paused. Then she pulled an envelope containing a few dried leaves and a jar of what appeared to be honey from her purse.

"We knew you were from Coloma, and that seemed almost like a sign. We were hoping you'd know more than us about the flower; that's what I thought you were talking about when you said 'my first animal.' I thought you were going to teach me something." The facial expression that punctuated that verb wasn't even sarcastic: there was genuine disappointment in it, which made Vik feel even worse than if she'd been mocking him. "We got your name from the Immigrant Assistance Center. There were only two people from the island, you and another woman, who died." She sighed and pointed to the Ploucquet within view of the kitchen. "As soon as I saw that poor rabbit, I knew we'd made a mistake. No dropout would ever make a career out of stuffing animals." She paused after saying this, as if she were deciding whether he deserved the next words to come out of her mouth. She seemed to think he did. "Of course, the idea isn't ours, it's much older. We're talking about a state of consciousness. Other drugs and experiences can produce it, too. I've always thought science was a mistake, that the mistake everyone made in the seventies and before was trying to convince the world with scientific arguments. It should be enough that beauty exists. It should be enough that courage exists. Some people talk about cosmic forces or communication with the animal world. Mine is always a spider. That's my form, my way of stepping back, of 'repairing cultural damage,' as Aero would say. Some people think there was a tribe here, too, that used the flower in its rituals, I don't know which of the strains. And then there was that commune in the sixties. They came up with this one," she said, stroking the leaves. "They probably brought it from your island decades ago."

As she spoke, she spread a bit of honey onto a slice of bread, picked up a few leaves, and sprinkled them on top.

"They taste bitter. It takes a while to get used to." Then, as if she were just remembering when and where the conversation was occurring, she looked into Vik's eyes and added, "I should have left a while ago, but I wanted to see where this could go."

"Right. You said they'd told you to be invisible."

"No one told me to do anything. Each one of us makes our own test. I chose this one: first in the street, then in the home of a man like you. Do you realize that more than fifteen people could live and eat comfortably in here? I've done the math. And all the food you waste . . . Please. But then, when you really think about it, everything in the world is just waste. No, I meant that I was curious how far you and I could go. What you would do after the cameras. That's what made me think you were a lost cause. I hadn't, before. Before, you didn't seem like a pig or bourgeois or an accomplice of the system—you have to have some sense of what you're doing to earn those stale adjectives. And you just seemed desperate. Do you know how many conversations you've had with another human being in the past few days? One. With the man who installed the cameras, of course. What's next? I asked myself. I could see you clear as day heading out to buy an assault rifle."

Pushing Vik's teacup to the side, she placed the bread with its supposed charge of enlightenment on his plate. A drop of honey slid down her hand (which was still dirty with that sticky kind of grime that advances in tacky patches, he thought). She licked it off, tucked a lock of hair behind her ear, and, apparently satisfied with her sermon, crossed her arms over her chest.

What was she hoping for? That he'd act like some character out of a movie? That a bite of bread would turn him into a rebel, a superhero, a wretch? This was probably just one more stop or test along the road she'd chosen for her coronation. There wasn't much difference between this woman and the religious fanatics who knocked on his door, Vik thought, disappointed. If he took all the extraordinary parts of the story away, if he took away all the coincidences, the ironies, and the flower, he would get the same thing as with any other group of humans with a cause: a lone, monstrous finger wagging in the air, and any individual will or intelligence annihilated by collectively clinging to a belief like a sordid raft.

Vik studied the woman carefully. Her hair had stopped dripping. He looked again at the network of wrinkles around her eyes. They weren't signs of age. Maybe they were the result of life out in the elements, since everything else (breasts, neck, and especially hands) seemed firm. No, he discarded the idea immediately. They weren't the result of life out in the elements, either. That woman had only been in the street or the woods for a little while. Her nails weren't damaged enough, and she didn't have the dry skin of the refugee women in Coloma. No, her skin had been moistened with creams and oils until very recently.

He regretted again not having paid more attention to the news about those people out there in the woods. He wondered if this woman had any children that she'd abandoned in order to shake society from its collective slumber. It was hard for him to imagine. But he hadn't imagined the dropouts would be so young, either. Come to think of it, some people defined youth exclusively as excess—a definition that, by nature, couldn't last beyond their thirties. But then again, he thought sarcastically, couldn't it just be that everyone in the world is thirty these days? Everyone but him. He remembered his expiration date perfectly: he had been twenty-four years old when his body began quitting on him. No, there hadn't been many excesses, not even before then.

They were signs of pain, he thought, returning to her wrinkles. Or what she understood as such. So it wouldn't be, or shouldn't be, he thought while counting the intervals between pulsations of the nerves in his back, impossible to convince her. Of what, not even he knew, but he'd discovered that he didn't want her out of his house. Not yet. At the mere thought of that group and its delirium of an alternative society, the pain, exhaustion, and annoyance collected in his fingertips as a tremor. He hid his hands under the table and went back to counting. After an interval of seventeen seconds, he retorted:

"And who says I don't have an assault rifle here?"

Without looking to see the effect of his remark, Vik laboriously got to his feet, trying not to be too obvious about using the table to hold himself up. She stood, as well. She looked astonished. Subdued, with her arms at her sides, she watched him struggle with his back's complaints. Vik counted his steps to the staircase, a distance he crossed by supporting himself on the furniture: thirty-nine, exactly. More than twice his average. The stairs themselves were easier: his quadriceps could do all the work.

Finally seated on the bed, he heard her moving around downstairs as he undressed. He listened more carefully, expecting to catch, from one moment to the next, the sound of his front door slamming. But that wasn't what happened. He heard the water running, chairs being moved around, drawers, glass, and metal in combinations that seemed almost absurd in their familiarity: the woman had washed, dried, and put away the dishes, and now she was climbing the stairs.

☞

They weren't ready. But they were never going to be. I know this now that it's all over, now that my hands are shaking, too. I'm repeating it for you, Dr. Danko, but also for myself. Do you think I've earned a few sedatives after the miracle in the cemetery? I'd say I have. And some lavender tea, some forgiveness, and an end to all this.

To this room, this old-age center, to this memory you'll probably label and archive just like all the others, before moving on to a different group of seniors in another city, another country. Thousands, millions of words saved for posterity, paid for with thousands and millions in subsidies so that brilliant minds like yours can take paid vacations with their kids at some ski resort. How many stories like mine have you collected without any real intention of anyone ever pressing Play on them again? Doesn't matter to me. I hope you enjoy your vacation in the mountains. And that no one hears my story. That really is walking away with the last word.

Sometimes I want to believe. In astrology, in DNA or biology, in anything that could explain how a circle that opened more than thirty years ago just closed so perfectly. But there's no need for mystical explanations. At the end of the day, it was Smithfield's desperate plan that brought about this resolution, this chance to break even. I'm beating around the bush? Maybe. But how directly would you tell the story of how you could have prevented a young woman's death, and instead you just stood there, watching her walk away with a rifle in her hands until she disappeared in the woods? Oh, I'm pretty sure you'd beat around the bush, too, for as many years as you get.

There. I said it. Frank always suspected it and never forgave me. Of course, there were mitigating circumstances, just like I told the police. That day, it wasn't only the Marlin that went missing. Celeste did, too. It was a cold, foggy morning. The air coming out of the woods was heavy and white and it surrounded the Clarke mansion. When I woke up, neither of them was in the room. It was hard to get moving. Later, after everything happened, I considered the possibility that Gabi had put something in my food the night before. My head was too heavy; it was as if someone had tied me to the bed with cords stretching out from the nape of my neck. But maybe not. Maybe I'd just had one too many. I don't remember. I can't remember everything. But I do remember very clearly the moment I crouched down to look for my left shoe and saw that the Marlin wasn't under the bed. I thought about Celeste, about her mother's empty stare, and my blood froze.

The house was still in shadows as the day peeked through, gray and rainy. Everyone else was still asleep. No one got up before ten at Bridgend, except the cosmic painter when he was inspired, or some kid who'd popped too many pills—it was common to go down to the living room and see some kind of spectacle—but never anyone who was actually awake.

Gabi's favorite places were the attic and the woods. I picked the attic. It was a big room with a bathroom at the far end that we used for sessions as a group. It was on a corner of the house and had big picture windows. The walls were covered in old pink-and-cream-colored paper. I climbed the stairs without making a sound. The door was ajar. I pushed it open. I hadn't been in that room for months. I knew Gabi and Gutierrez had been doing experiments up there. But that day, all I found were bags of dirt, a few gardening tools scattered around, and a bunch of dead plants that had been ripped from their pots: whatever had grown there once wasn't growing anymore.

I didn't stop to think about that. Trust me, the last thing on my mind was the mystery of the flowers. On one of the sofas, I caught a glimpse of Celeste's yellow blanket under a pile of pillows, rags, and newspapers. I remembered hearing her cry in my sleep. I imagined Gabi bringing her up to the attic, imagined that in an attempt to calm her she'd suffocated her under those pillows. I thought all that with my hand still on the doorknob, paralyzed. It's amazing how much the mind can do in a few seconds, how much more than the body. I finally managed to pry myself from the door and lift up the pillows and rags. No, Celeste wasn't there. Desperate, I went over to the window that faced out front. There was Gabi, standing right at the line where the Clarke family's garden became the woods. She had the girl pressed against her left shoulder and the rifle in her right hand. I remember it vividly, the blue pleated dress she was wearing, the white sweater, the canvas sneakers. The deer was right behind her. She'd released it, but it still followed her at a distance, disoriented after so many months in captivity. I saw it sniff the air and pause, looking at the woods like someone about to step into a party.

I didn't hesitate this time. I ran down the stairs not caring how much noise I made with my shoes, my breathing, my thoughts. I went out the back door and into the garden, and I swear it wasn't ten seconds before I'd caught up to her and grabbed the girl from her arms.

Gabi looked at me with eyes that suddenly weren't vacant

or begging for completion. There was peace there. The peace of someone who's thought all they're going to think, who's reached the outer limit of thinking, where thinking retreats and there's only room for action.

"Much better, Berilia," she said in a voice just as serene, her eyes on the baby I was clutching to my chest. And then she added something I'll never forget: "Time to get cleaned up and buy some butter."

With a perfect smile on her face, she ran toward the deer, which was a few steps ahead by then and had been standing there, watching us. When it saw her approach, it charged into the thicket.

Every time I go back to that scene in my memory, I hold Celeste in the crook of one arm and reach out with the other to grab Gabi by the shoulder or the elbow, or even by the dress. I confirm every single time that yes, it would have been possible. But I didn't do it. I've said it before. What matters is what a person does, not what she says.

They never found the deer. But I'm sure I heard two shots. I've always thought that Gabi meant to go without leaving anything behind that could be called hers. It was only by accident she didn't destroy those plants. The logical thing would have been for Celeste and the deer to go the same route. Maybe the animal survived. Or maybe she simply had the foresight to fire once in the air to make sure the rifle was loaded properly before placing it—with an aptitude that surprises me to this day—in the exact position for the bullet to be fatal.

But those details don't matter now. What matters is that I did absolutely nothing. I stood there in the garden feeling the girl's heart beating against mine for what felt like forever but couldn't have been more than a few seconds. I eventually pulled her away from my chest and looked in her eyes. That was when I knew I'd done the right thing: those were Frank Smithfield's eyes and, if it was up to me, I was going to make sure they stayed open as long as possible.

☜

It started to drizzle on the way back. Mr. Müller cursed his lack of preparation: his stomach was growling but he didn't have a cereal bar on him. He hadn't even taken the precaution of bringing a flashlight along. Once he managed to put the densest part of the woods behind him, he decided to enter the city through the north end of the cemetery, which would surely be well lit. He'd need to cross the whole place, following its asphalt paths up and down its two hills and orienting himself by the mausoleums until he made it through the gate on Grandville. It was the only way not to get lost. He'd been thinking about all this, and about the foreigner's speech, about how the power of his voice and his stature contrasted so starkly with his flimsy words. None of it impressed him any more than a suit of armor on display in a museum; they were a record of a bygone war, or a shield that had proved totally useless for winning it, in any event. And what in God's name did he mean with that "strategy for living an organic life" business? Was there perhaps a non-carbon-based form of life he wasn't aware of? Mr. Müller hated those redundancies meant to sound scientific, like those people who go on about "natural electrolytes." Talk about not having even the most basic grasp of chemistry.

Carbon, chemistry, and the dead people he'd been walking over—quickly, to avoid getting wet—made him wonder what the active substance in albaria was, what molecule it was that transformed that group of young people, that supposedly brought them back to a place where an animal brother guided them away from words and their limitations. Trying to understand, Mr. Müller recalled the faces in the circle that had formed around the foreigner. In particular, he remembered two boys who seemed younger than the rest of the group and who were clearly related: they had identical noses, curly brown hair, and some baby fat still clinging to their cheeks. They couldn't have been eighteen yet, but they seemed ready for anything, just the same. One had a bandage around the tip of his left ring finger; the other, one covering his right eye. At first, Mr. Müller thought it must have been a sign of strength: to survive a wound like that shows a soldier is ready for war. But others around the circle were bandaged as well, so he concluded that the bandages were either symbolic or had something to do with the effects of albaria on the bodies of those who were a bit too assiduous in their consumption.

Then he remembered a passage he hadn't paid much attention to when he'd read it in Lund's book a few months earlier. It could well be that the active substance in the leaves of the plant was like ergot fungus, which caused, in some cases, a loss of circulation in the extremities. But it didn't seem likely. The dropouts seemed healthy, and showed no signs of the gangrene found in those affected by St. Anthony's fire. Maybe they'd read Lund, as well, and had bandaged themselves in honor of that tribe, which apparently practiced ritual mutilation. Or maybe they just wanted to symbolize something. Their fragility, thought Mr. Müller. The fragility or uselessness of the human animal in the face of all other living beings. No, not their fragility. Their vulnerability, he thought in a burst of unsatisfactory inspiration that coincided with his arrival at the Klink obelisk. Maybe that's why those people were obsessed with deer. The albaria offered them a way back to that mute world they believed was simpler, wiser. Mr. Müller sighed and leaned against a pine. He decided that the only way to find out, to see what this "spiritual resistance" was really about, was to try the albaria leaves he'd put in his refrigerator a few days earlier. He felt better after arriving, if not at a conclusion, then at least at an experiment that might bring him closer to one, and decided to celebrate with a cigarette, only his third in an eventful day. Not bad for someone who had started trying to quit ten years ago, when his wife died of cancer and the price of a pack went through the roof.

The rain had slowed, only a few drops were falling on his hat and the fisherman's raincoat he'd had the presence of mind to put on, following his daily consultation of the weather forecast. He lit the cigarette, inhaled the tobacco mixed with rain and pine, and exhaled through his nose, noticing how, even after all those years, the first puff still made his head spin.

Unlike many of his classmates at the university, Mr. Müller had never been much of a drug enthusiast. Back then, many of the biochemistry students picked that major with the secret objective of becoming specialists in the identification of psychoactive mushrooms and flowers, a knowledge that more than a few combined with extreme sports or a passion for rock climbing and trekking to unknown places. Like Teddy Gutierrez, a young man with thick glasses, brown hair, and a beard, who always wore a brown-checked jacket and matching pants—a uniform that didn't manage to make him look as dignified as he intended. He could wear a blazer all he wanted, but Teddy Gutierrez was always going to look like he'd just escaped from a fire with his meager belongings in the overstuffed reddish leather folio he kept with him at all times. At university, they called him the Priest. Not because he'd gone to seminary, but because he always sounded as if he was about to launch into prayer, and for his composure and restrained manners, which had been refined during a grim childhood no one knew much about. From the time he was very young, people wanted him to hear their confessions. The slightly curved spine, the impenetrable eyes behind those overly thick glasses, and the flat nose down which they inevitably slid, forcing a corrective movement of the hand, all inspired trust. That movement, which looked suited to someone preparing for a fight, became a trademark of his personality over the years, the gesture of a serious and focused man, with his ring finger holding up his glasses or pressing his pineal gland, his third eye, or whatever other clairvoyant channel prepared him for listening. This gesture was inexplicably successful with the ladies. Or at least that's what young Müller thought. He'd belonged to the group of serious, entrepreneurial students who didn't see much romance but who did end up owning their own businesses.

Teddy Gutierrez, on the other hand, never even graduated: he'd opted to travel around and experience in his own body what others only dared to read about in books. He wanted to catalog the different kinds of hallucinations associated with each psychoactive substance. He started with the personal diary of his trips and continued his research in groups. He even got the Klink family and other philanthropists to finance part of the project. In that phase of his "research," his work consisted of recording the visions of various subjects under the influence of different drugs. You'd see him from time to time on campus, carrying an enormous tape recorder and recruiting students for his "consciousness experiments." That's what he called them. Mr. Müller remembered hearing him present some of the results once: they seemed like the ravings of a prophet. They'd reminded him of Swedenborg's extravagant, ridiculous—and, above all, exceedingly boring—project of classifying angels.

There was something arrogant in privileging experience over experiment that way, thought young Müller, who believed back then that scientists should only resort to self-experimentation when there was no other way to obtain the desired knowledge. Just as he was doing now, having decided to try albaria for lack of any other way to understand what was going on out there in the woods. The decision made him feel younger, and it was that idea of putting his own body on the line that had made him think of Gutierrez as the drizzle falling on his raincoat gradually turned to mist. That, and the Klink family obelisk. The fact that Berenice had just showed him a photo of his former classmate with other members of his group was simply the perfect way to close the circle of his musings.

Still leaning against the tree, he took one last puff of his cigarette, crushed it out carefully against the bark, and stuck the butt in his pocket. He was always mindful about that: careless smokers had already caused several fires in the area. The woods were getting more dangerous; it was nothing like when he was a child. You used to be able to wander around these valleys for hours without running into another person; now they were full of homeless people who went from one city to the next, trying to escape the winter or find towns with more compassionate police officers. Then there were groups like the self-proclaimed "dropouts." Not even the local fauna was the same. There was an outcry over the slow but steady extinction of several bird species due to this latest human advance (not the advances of production or capitalism: the advance of the abject and the self-ostracized) into nature's territory. Mr. Müller didn't pay too much attention to these protests, but it was true that the deer had acted strangely during the summer. He remembered things he'd seen on the local news: A man attacked in his vegetable garden by a huge, ferocious buck. And Helga, an orphaned doe one family had raised from a fawn; as the two eldest children walked her back from grazing in the mountains, the docile animal broke into a gallop and launched itself at the windshield of a van. The driver was killed instantly, and they'd had to put Helga down. It was strange, a doe attacking like that, especially one without fawns, and the episode was added to the disconcerting list of cases of "animal insanity."

Mr. Müller peeled himself away from the tree he'd been using to protect himself from the last of the raindrops. The sky had begun to clear, letting through a few rays of moonlight. That was when he saw, off to one side of the Klink family mausoleums, the gravestone marked with the name Cecilia Brown. He felt his thoughts speeding up, racing, rejecting certain paths and choosing others. Why was that name so familiar? It took him a few seconds more to understand that it was the same last name as his renter's, and only then was he able to find the mental shortcut he'd been missing. He remembered that Helga's owners lived relatively close to the cemetery where Emma had told him she'd been able to grow her first and only albaria—purely by chance, after scattering the seeds over the grave of her grandmother, Cecilia Brown.

"If only I could reproduce that moment of pure and absolute mental clarity," Mr. Müller said to Berenice, who had stopped listening to him a long time ago and was now dreaming about motorcycles and recklessness with her head resting on her left elbow. "A moment of true intellectual splendor, I'd say. I don't think I've felt anything like it since my student days."

Because in that moment, still in the cemetery and staring at the headstone of a woman he'd never met, he had deciphered the secret of the albaria plant: the only way to get its seeds to sprout in that climate was by passing them through a deer's stomach first, which broke down their thick protective film and allowed them to germinate. It was the only possible explanation, because it also coincided with another detail in Lund's diary: the fact that the tribe of seers he described had kept wild turkeys. He was probably talking about hoatzins or cuckoos, which have stomachs like a ruminant's and could have broken down the seeds. That must be how albaria could grow on the continent, the same way the seeds that Emma threw on her grandmother's grave had germinated. Some animals must have eaten them along with the grass. And maybe they'd nibbled on the plant's leaves once they started growing indiscriminately around the whole cemetery. That would explain the madness of the deer over the summer, the unusually violent episodes that had made it into the papers.

He was certain the dropouts had also reached this conclusion. That's why they had deer inside the hotel. They must have been feeding them seeds in the hope of producing more plants. Come to think of it, it was a little disappointing that their interest in the deer was so material, and ultimately had nothing to do with the "spiritual resistance" they preached so energetically.

But none of that really mattered to Mr. Müller. What mattered to him was proving that, despite his age, despite his failed business and the emphysema creeping into his lungs, he was always going to be one step ahead of the Teddy Gutierrezes of the world, no matter how much they tried to reinvent themselves as repentant executives. Yes, man is a beast to man. But not even a wolf, just some generic animal lost in the contemplation of a retouched image of itself that it tried, unsuccessfully, to connect with the "natural" world. A fake innocence, chemically induced. An artificial savage. None of that could compare to having a clear mind, a sharpened blade at the service of real survival. And Mr. Müller was sure he had one.

12

He heard her enter the closet, crinkle shopping bags, open or close zippers. Lying on his side to ease the pressure on his back (he'd resisted the urge to take a spoonful of morphine), he considered the possibility that she was gathering her things to leave. It didn't seem so. Could she be getting ready to spend the night on her shelf? Like a hen in a nest box? The image made him convulse with laughter ill-suited to the condition of his nerves. He knew he had dashed her expectations. A poor invalid, or a brute armed and ready to defend his right to private property, was the role she'd assigned him in this play of hers. As if the happy years he'd spent in Coloma, his acceptance of the disease his body had chosen for its rebellion, and a natural disaster that turned him into yet another immigrant in this city he detested could fit within either of the two variables to which she'd reduced his name.

He'd show her soon enough just how complex and unpredictable a real human being could be, he thought, clenching his fists under the pillow. How terribly empathetic he could be, unlike her and those imbeciles in the woods. True ethics can't exist in a group, only between two peers. He would teach her this patiently, elegantly. He would cook for her, give her his bed, and sleep on the chaise longue downstairs. He would get her some better clothes. He would confide the secrets of his past in Coloma, secrets that would slowly reveal something else: the idea that she and she alone was destined to share this suspended time in a northern city with him. He would convince her she was beautiful, unique, indispensable. He could do it. And once he said those words, there would be no turning back. Then, when she felt loved and protected, that's when they'd see just how much she cared about changing the world. They'd see who walked away the winner, thought Vik, unclenching his fists and giving in with a smile to the pillow's softness.

He had a short dream about the museum. He was inside one of the displays, but it didn't look like one of Smithfield's dioramas; the mannequins were damaged and wet, the paint that tried to pass itself off as skin was falling off in chunks, and the sad white plaster of truth sat exposed under the yellow glow of the lights. There were many of them, more than ten, placed near the glass in a way that didn't compose any particular scene. There was no one else in the museum and he walked among the Indians with a portable radio broadcasting a championship hockey match. There was a leak somewhere. Suddenly his feet were fighting against the water and his radio had become a rifle, though he could still hear the announcer's voice. The water quickly rose to his waist and the mannequins, which were nailed to the floor and were now the size of children (actually, they were children), began to drown. Not him. He was too tall to be in any danger in that half-flooded display. He could feel the water between his legs like a caress that turned into heat and gradually brought him back to his bed, to the vague awareness of not being alone, of the woman's soft and capable hand moving over his sex.

She was lying at his side with her mouth in the hollow between his neck and the pillow; her body resting on his, she covered him with her breath as well. It was her left hand that was doing all the work. And with remarkable skill. He pictured her closing the tap in the bath, spreading honey on a slice of bread, and yes, she had used that same hand. Thinking about those details and about the morphine patch he still wore on his shoulder helped delay what came next. He was the first to be surprised at how quickly he responded to the stimulation despite his exhaustion, his pain, and all the chemicals. He had a few seconds to think, or rather to hesitate, before that inevitable and long-postponed violence took over completely. He rolled over and took the woman's breasts in his hands; she parted her lips and let out a slightly louder moan. No. He wasn't going to do it, he thought. If he did, the act would belong to the short and incidental time of instinct, not to true recognition. He wasn't going to let her win that easily. Faking a groan of pain, he collapsed at her side. He stroked her hair and looked into her eyes with an intensity that could just as well have been love, empathy, or a scientist's fascination with an object of study.

"Not yet," he said, without taking his eyes off her.

He saw her smile, either out of happiness, it seemed, or in anticipation of a greater victory. Her arms, stretched across the pillows, her body—with its short and slightly thick torso—lit by the midday sun, her smile, and especially her eyes, which looked at him with intimacy that implied years of nights spent together, all seemed to indicate her abandon. It almost bothered him that it was so easy, that she'd succumbed so meekly to masculine dominance. He sat on the edge of the bed. Without taking his eyes off her, he dressed and reached over to the cigarette box on his nightstand.

"What happened to the girl?" he heard her ask, still on her

back, but now with her arms folded behind her head and her face turned slightly in the direction of his arm, perhaps (yes, definitely) hoping to be caressed.

Vik decided to humor her. Sometimes, when the pain was constant, acute, and unfathomable, it endowed him with moments of clairvoyance. Moments when his counting slowed to the point that reality, tiny and predictable, could sneak into his calculations. He slid his thumb along the contour of the woman's ear. It was too big for her face, a mark of vulgarity even in Coloma. Her smile widened.

She wanted a love story. It didn't even have to be about Tania, anyone would do. A story she could use to shield herself from what had just happened, that could explain his rejection of her or at least suggest that he was, after all, something more than a man whose interest in the world and its cycles was shattered exactly seventeen years ago.

Without taking his eyes off her, he lit the cigarette, inhaled, and counted five seconds before answering.

"She disappeared. In the eruption."

He shouldn't have told her the canary story. He saw clearly now that the only lasting victory was anonymity; that was why the woman lying in his bed had chosen to lose herself in a group. Yes, in that group, more than in any hallucination those substances could produce. What a relief it must be, the chance to get lost inside something bigger than herself, thought Vik as the memory—of all the medical offices he'd visited in Kent, the acceptance letters from prestigious foreign universities tossed on what had once been his father's table, the faded paint around the window through which he watched thin black smoke rise into the sky over the island—filled the silence that followed Tania's return and hung in the overly heated air of his bedroom in that northern city.

There hadn't been more than eighteen fatalities in the eruption, all of them in the town of Soufrière Coeur. Kent had been evacuated swiftly and efficiently. But Tania—who'd filled out considerably, had painted her long nails, and had started wearing tight dresses men couldn't ignore—wasn't in the city when the precautionary measures were taken. She was with her crew of boys in the mountains. The boys did most of the work, from picking to processing and preserving; the ones she chose got younger and younger and her only condition was that they not consume the plant. A few of them slept on the veranda, which had been closed in with glass. The only bird that had survived her childhood passion was the macaw, which lived in her bedroom for years. Its successors learned to say the same word in English, French, and Spanish.

Tania had tried to leave the city with as many albaria plants as possible (all attempts to grow it artificially had failed, even those of the first explorers to visit Coloma, hundreds of years ago). Even Mr. Cardelús was worried about his daughter. At least, he was as worried as he could allow himself to be. Vik ran into him on the dock where he'd gone to help with the evacuation. Cardelús was old and fat, almost blind from diabetes. It had been years since he left the business—which had never made him rich, or at least not rich enough—in Tania's hands. He had two suitcases and three cardboard boxes with him, far more than evacuees were permitted. He said that he'd waited two whole days for his daughter. But the city was covered in ash. How much longer could he wait? Vik rushed to absolve him. He hadn't thought about Tania in a long time. He hadn't thought about anything except diagnoses and treatments in a long time.

He decided not to tell the woman any of that. He opted instead for drama, inventing a long story of unrequited love, years of patient waiting, accidental encounters, rebuffs, and silent adoration. He topped it all off with his rescue attempt, amid the smoke and ash, against the human avalanche descending the mountain that day. He'd never learned to drive; his household had always had drivers, but there he was—aboard an army vehicle he'd gotten his hands on because of his last name, still capable of desperate acts and of asserting his privilege. Or, better yet, with newfound temerity, a side effect of facing his illness. He made sure to include only a few details that made the story more believable. He borrowed a stampede of cattle from a story he'd heard from a family who lived in the mountains; he got the death toll (based on disappearances reported by relatives, not on the number of bodies recovered) from a report he'd read in the refugee camp where he'd spent just four days, the time it took Prasad to pull some strings and have him moved to the continent.

The woman rested her hand on his. There weren't tears in her eyes, exactly; it was more like a viscous sheath of understanding.

That feeling of triumphant disgust from the dream about winning the Ping-Pong tournament had returned. He hadn't thought of Tania since the eruption—that is, he hadn't thought about the chubby young woman who sold albaria, mushrooms, and other hallucinogenic substances. He didn't care whether she was alive or dead. But over the course of that day, that duel with his intruder, he'd managed to rid himself of the other one, of the girl who loved birds. And along with her, all of Coloma and the disaster that—it didn't take a genius to recognize it—had actually changed his life for the better. For the first time in years, he even thought a bit fondly about Prasad.

"I'll tell you my story, too," said the woman. She rolled over to face the window and crossed her arms over her chest, as if she needed to hug herself in order to speak.

She began with the day, nine years earlier, when she'd left her parents' home on the other side of the river. She didn't even notice that Vik had gotten out of bed. She just kept building her story, which was plagued by flourishes (who cared if they lived in a trailer park?) and what she must have believed were major traumas (she couldn't have been the only obese, unpopular girl at her school). She dedicated precious minutes to digressions meant to convince him that the institution known as family was the psychological, philosophical, and sociological equivalent of hell. That's what the dictionary definition would be if linguists were actually scientific and honest, she said, her voice wavering as she choked back tears that Vik found melodramatic. "Family. Noun. Pain or the social administration of such," she recited in what appeared to be, judging by the inflections he could still make out from the hallway, the climax of her sermon (her story had quickly turned into one). Confronted with that truth, which had so long been hidden behind commercials for washing machines, televisions, and diapers, she said, the only option was to reject it all and run away, build something different, pure (to her, "pure" meant "natural" or, even worse, "animal," thought Vik as he passed the closet).

She was still talking about how all that—the construction of a different kind of society—didn't mean giving up love, but just the opposite, and about how the flowers and the leaders had appeared in a second phase and weren't even the most important part of the "spiritual economy of the group." She'd begun to sound drowsy, so much so that Vik wondered, still in the hallway, if she hadn't eaten a few leaves when she was in the closet earlier.

He still had time to go to the bathroom and take a spoonful of morphine, congratulating himself for keeping a bottle in every room of the house. Then he went downstairs as slowly and quietly as he could and sat on the chaise. When he felt the solace of the opioid envelop him, he pulled the phone from his pocket and looked at the first images he'd seen of the woman. She didn't seem like a child or a threatening presence covered in hair anymore. She seemed like what she was: a poor girl tired of the comforts into which she'd been born. He considered this as he came up with his story. When it was ready, he opened his phone and dialed the three numbers. Pressing the buttons, he felt a new kind of vertigo, a triumphant rise in his heart or in his voice, which was finally recognized as that of a Bob or a Tom by the police who picked up his call right away.

✿

That was the end of everything: no one wanted to rehearse for the Big Concert anymore, no one could. We didn't speak for days. Frank got his things and went to his mother's house. A little while later, he accepted Gutierrez's invitation to travel around Central America. That's when he invented his tribe of Primevals. Clarke moved out to the West Coast, where he opened a surf shop and later founded a successful film and television production company. The rest of the kids went back to their homes, to boredom, to work. Like me. They gave me a job somewhere peaceful where time stands still, where there's no room for variation. Or that's what I thought. Because you can't hide from those things, not even in a museum. Or in a cemetery. Come to think of it, there's not much difference.

I mentioned that we'd had a session up near Amarillo Hill to practice tracking. It went pretty well, which is why I decided we'd go back there this past Saturday. I taught them how to see. That's one of the hardest things, Doctor. To look at a tree, for example, and see the dozens of creatures that have been there. To find the holes left by a woodpecker, the path of a squirrel around its trunk, the tracks of a fox nearby. You could do the same exercise with any park bench. I do it all the time: I see the newspaper left behind by a drifter rather than a casual reader, a runner's bottle of juice, a child's bubblegum, the trace of a couple in love. But most people are blind to all this, to the signs that could save them one day. That's why they're such easy targets: they have too much faith in institutions, in the police, in their jobs and their friends. Yeah, that's what I told them that day before we headed out for our last training session.

After a few observation exercises, we broke off into two groups. The Armstrong sisters and Max Cercone in one, Mr. and Mrs. Paz and Elizabeth in the other. It had snowed that morning, just a dusting but perfect for the exercise. If there were deer in the area, we were definitely going to find tracks. I decided to join the second group: since our first class, Elizabeth had struck me as the unstable one and I'd decided to keep a close eye on her. I was wrong about that, too.

No one was supposed to fire a single shot. Looking back on it, I can see it was a little naïve of me to think they wouldn't, when they were all dying to debut their social utility and recently acquired rifles. All I asked them to do was to come back with the movements of a deer traced out on a map, with a few leaves or flowers bearing bite marks, with a few droppings; ideally, with a photo of the almond-shaped hoofprints I'd taught them to identify in our first session.

There wasn't time for any of that. I don't know what happened with the first group, who were assigned the opposite side of the hill. I joined Elizabeth and Mr. and Mrs. Paz. If everything went as planned, we'd meet the others behind Concordia Cemetery.

We walked for more than forty minutes. Betty was already showing signs of agitation, so I suggested we take a break. We were talking about that, and about the possibility that we'd need to cancel the exercise if it started to snow again. Elizabeth had gone ahead to check for signs on the trunk of a maple. You could already see the tombs from there; the terrain rose and fell again over by the cemetery, where the trees thinned out. I gestured to her to wait, but she was immersed in her task and her eyes were glued to the tree. I was about to call out to her and break the silence—violating the most sacred rule of the woods—when something raced between us. I say "something" because all I saw was a white spot and long black hair flying in the wind. I hadn't yet reached the conclusion that what I was looking at was a woman when I heard a shot, then another, and then a man shouting and cries of alarm. I got to the other side of the hill as quickly as I could. Tom was right behind me. It didn't occur to us to follow the woman: the two of us instinctively headed toward the shots and the voices and almost ran smack into Max Cercone's bright red face and, a little farther, the two police officers on their way up the hill from the cemetery.

"I got him. I got him," Max repeated, like a madman. "I know it. He was huge, at least eight points."

It was true. There were deer tracks on the path, probably from a sizable buck. But Max hadn't hit a thing. The police, on the other hand, had. When he heard the shot, one of them had drawn his standard-issue sidearm and now the woman in white was leaving a trail of blood on the snow as she ran. I was able to capture pieces of all this as I listened to the older of the two police officers shouting at Max, shouting at all of us for hunting in a restricted area. By then, the Armstrong sisters had arrived. They were carrying pieces of flowers and leaves and smiling like star pupils, completely oblivious to what had just happened. I felt the eyes of the whole group fall on me. They wanted me to absolve them, or at least to deal with the policeman. Betty Paz opened the seat her husband had been carrying for her that whole time and sank into it, staring at the moss-covered angel on the nearest tomb. I saw Elizabeth bring her hands to her mouth and turned my head in the direction of her anguished expression, and that's when the younger officer appeared, carrying the woman. I don't know if she was still breathing. I don't think so, because the whole top of her dress was stained with blood. It seemed as if she'd been hit in the neck or the clavicle, but I couldn't tell for sure because just as I was about to get closer, just as I was about to make the mistake of speaking, of trying to reason with a group of desperate seniors and two police officers too nervous for the job, I felt a hand close around mine. I looked down and saw the eyes of Frank Smithfield, of Celeste, of a little girl who looked up at me and said the most absurd and also the most lucid thing I've heard in the last thirty years:

"Hi. My name is Berenice Brown. Would you like to be my relative?"

I took another look at the scene still unfolding around me. I saw the two police officers bent over the woman; I scanned the face of each of my students, one by one; I even paused to observe the crosses and angels on the tombs down in the hollow. Only then could I see myself. Not as a wayward old woman, off course since 1969. I saw myself as what I am, Doctor: one more passenger in the greatest shipwreck any era, any country, any generation has known; someone who survived the sound of a thousand and one doors locking, too late and

too hard. I saw myself as what I was, and what I am: Beryl Hope, survivor. And so, full of a feeling I can only describe as gratitude, I met the girl's eyes, squeezed her hand, and said:
"Yes."

෨

When Berenice woke up, Saturday morning was well underway and snow as fine as confectioner's sugar was falling outside. Thinking about it made her hungry again. She turned over on the cot where Mr. Müller had tucked her in under two moss-green blankets he must have brought from his house. He'd also left a thermos, which appeared to contain coffee, on the table, along with some plain rolls and a jar of marmalade.

But it wasn't enough, thought Berenice, because before he left, before he picked her up out of the chair and deposited her on the cot, Mr. Müller had spoken to her in the same voice he would use when he needed to get Sissy to take her blood-pressure medicine. "You can sleep here tonight, that's fine," he'd said. "Tomorrow, we'll see." She knew what that meant. "Tomorrow, we'll see" meant "This is just for today," or "Don't get excited," or something like that. "Tomorrow, we'll see" meant "Your uncle's on his way," and also "This shop is mine and don't go holding your breath for your mother to come back to run it again or to take you away with her."

There was a reason Emma Lynn always used to say that Mr. Müller was jealous of them, that his obsession with spying on them was a way of having a life again, an excuse to turn off the television for a while and see what other people did with their time. Not even his two children spoke to him. They'd moved away the minute they turned eighteen and never visited, not even on his birthday or during the holidays. Berenice could see why. Mr. Müller was like an old tree ravaged by disease or parasites that managed to stay standing when all that was left was the bark. Berenice always thought of the word "hollow" when she saw him. No. He wasn't going to last much longer. That's what Berenice was thinking as she bit into a dry piece of bread. All around her, the plants demanded her attention. The dahlias were drooping and the chrysanthemums were begging for water. What a relief to not have to be part of all this effort, to not have to care for the things Emma Lynn abandoned without a second thought. Just the idea of going to look for her in the woods or the broken-heart hotel exhausted Berenice so much that she had to lay her head back down on the pillow. She didn't have the strength for it. But she didn't have another plan, either. It was time for a trip to the cemetery.

Purple Queen was where she'd left her, with her bud intact. The lack of water hadn't affected her in the least. Berenice put her in a tote bag, along with the gray notebook and the two remaining rolls. She took one last look at her mother's business, opened the door, and headed for the Sphinxes.

Following the ritual Emma Lynn had taught her, she took the long way, a path that went up and down hills and ended at Mr. Winter's mausoleum, where the cemetery met the woods. It was made of white granite and was as big as a temple. Five steps led up to the entryway, which had a column on each side. She walked until she reached the two statues with breasts like a woman's on the body of a lion. By that time, it had stopped snowing and a white light glowed between the clouds, announcing it was noon.

She sat between the two Sphinxes and took a bite of one of the rolls, even though she wasn't hungry anymore. She did it just so she wouldn't be sitting there with her arms crossed. *Crossing your arms is giving up*, she thought. Eating, on the other hand, was holding on to what you believe. It was something

Halley always said: that eating was an act of faith, which is why you had to be careful about what you put in your mouth. The act was too powerful.

She hadn't even swallowed her first mouthful when she heard voices. At first she thought they were coming from the tomb, so she stood up and walked around it to the left. She heard footsteps and branches snapping. A woman dressed in white crossed the gravel path at a sprint, jumped over a stone coffin, and ran into the woods. Two police officers were right behind her. Much farther away, at the top of the hill, a man with a cane was gripping his head with his free hand.

Berenice heard one, no, two shots. Still holding the bag with Purple Queen, she set off toward the woods along a path covered in leaves.

There were people on the hill. They were old and seemed agitated, as if they'd been running to catch a train and had just missed it. A man was standing with his back to Berenice, holding a rifle and repeating, "I got him, I got him," and a really tall lady was staring at the bark of a tree. Two more old women came from the other direction with flowers in their hands. Berenice heard more voices and something that sounded like a radio. She gathered that someone over there was speaking with authority, almost yelling; she couldn't see well, but it was probably one of the police officers. He seemed to be arguing with the man who was still holding his rifle with both hands and another one, a little taller and more wrinkled, who'd arrived a bit later. But none of that mattered to Berenice, because she'd just found in that group what she'd been looking for since the first night she slept alone in the apartment on Edmond Street.

She was old, too. But she was different. She was wearing a violet tracksuit and her white curls were mussed by the wind;

leaning on her rifle, she observed the others through black-framed glasses. There was a strength and serenity in her eyes that Berenice had never seen before. The woman had seen it all, and nothing had shaken or shocked her. That's what Berenice was thinking as she walked toward her with long, confident strides, indifferent to what the police or the others were saying, indifferent to everything but the feeling that the knot she'd had in her chest for days was finally coming loose.

If anyone had asked her, she would have said that the woman was her mother, her father, her grandmother, her aunt, and her sister.

AUTHOR'S NOTE

Part of the creative process that nourished the writing of this novel was going through stories that appeared in the international press between 2008 and 2012. From the woman who hid in a stranger's house in Japan, to deer attacks in the United States, to other episodes in Russia, Mexico, Scotland, and Argentina, these stories informed the ones I was imagining. Among the films, literary works, testimonials, and internet sources I consulted, the following proved especially useful and inspiring: *Slouching Towards Bethlehem*, by Joan Didion; *Droppers: America's First Hippie Commune*, by Mark Matthews; *Still Life: Adventures in Taxidermy*, by Melissa Milgrom; *Explorations of the Highlands of the Brazil*, by Sir Richard Burton; and *Hallucinogens and Culture*, by Peter T. Furst. I'm grateful to these authors for having shared their knowledge and experience.

I would also like to thank Ramiro Freudenthal, Ariadna Castellarnau, Carina González, Irene Klein, Gabriela Franco, María Julia Rossi, Graciela Gliemmo, and Paola Lucantis, who read early versions of this novel or discussed details of its plot with me. I'm very fortunate to have them in my life.

Finally, my sincerest thanks to Madeline Jones, editor at Henry Holt, and to Heather Cleary for her beautiful translation.

Buenos Aires, April 2020

About the Author

Betina González is an Argentine fiction writer. She holds a PhD in Hispanic literatures from the University of Pittsburgh and an MFA in bilingual creative writing from the University of Texas at El Paso. She teaches creative writing at New York University in Buenos Aires and the University of Buenos Aires. She was awarded the Clarín Prize for *Arte menor*, her first novel, and the Tusquets Award for *Las poseídas*. Her other books include the bestselling collection *El amor es una catástrofe natural*, *Juegos de playa*, and *América alucinada*, her first work to be published in English, as *American Delirium*.

About the Translator

Heather Cleary's translations include poetry and prose by María Ospina, Roque Larraquy, Brenda Lozano, Sergio Chejfec, and Oliverio Girondo; her work has been recognized or supported by the National Book Foundation, the Best Translated Book Awards, the Mellon Foundation, and the Banff International Literary Translation Centre. A member of the Cedilla & Co. translation collective, she has served as a judge for various national translation awards, and is a founding editor of the digital, bilingual *Buenos Aires Review*. She teaches at Sarah Lawrence College.